Starlight Magic

Books by Suzie O'Connell

NORTHSTAR
First Instinct
Mountain Angel
Summer Angel
Twice Shy
Once Burned
Mistletoe Kisses
Starlight Magic
Wild Angel
Forgotten Angel
Last Surrender

TWO-LANE WYOMING
The Road to Garrett

SEA GLASS COVE
The Abalone Shell
The Driftwood Promise

www.suzieoconnell.com

Starlight Magic

A Northstar Novel

SUZIE O'CONNELL

SUNSET
Rose
BOOKS

Copyright © 2016 Suzie O'Connell

All rights reserved. No portion of this book may be copied, retransmitted, reposted, duplicated, or otherwise used without the express written approval of the author, except by reviewers who may quote brief excerpts in connection with a review.

This is a work of fiction. Names, characters, places, and incidents are either the product of the author's imagination or used fictitiously, and any resemblance to actual persons, living or dead, business establishments, events, or locales is entirely coincidental.

ISBN-13: 978-1-950813-06-3

*In loving memory of my grandfather, "Ferg" Ferguson,
one of the brightest stars in my life.*

*Every day I sit down to write, his encouragement to chase
my dream echoes in my heart.*

I love you and miss you. Always.

One

IT WASN'T THE SPLIT LIP, the bruised cheek and accompanying black eye, or the angry red marks on her throat, nor was it the ragged, chin-length bob maniacally chopped in the bathroom of the police station after noticing the blood caked in the long, lustrous raven waves. It was the hollow, haunted gaze without a spark of life that had made her unrecognizable.

Celeste compared the memory of the woman who had looked back at her two months ago to the one scrutinizing her now. The lip had healed and the bruises had faded, and she'd had her hair neatened up by a professional into a stylish bob that suited her face, but the eyes were still as empty. Occasionally, rage would ignite them or a distant grief would claw through the numbness to fill them with tears that spilled silently and unnoticed down her cheeks, but mostly, they remained lifeless, like now. The woman in this mirror was more recognizable than the one in that other reflection but only because she'd become familiar. She caught herself searching for traces of the woman she'd been before that night and found none. That woman was as dead as her husband.

She squeezed a generous puddle of gel into her palm and worked it through her hair until it was all smoothed back from her face. Then, to her ensemble of black pleather pants and matching tank top, knee-high black boots with three-inch heels, she added the final piece—a pair of dark-tinted, oval sunglasses with thin, black wire frames that hid her spiritless eyes. Black on black on black. Utterly colorless.

Like me, now.

With a growl, she spun away from the mirror and strode out of the bathroom, flipping the lights off on her way.

She adjourned to the main living area of the house she'd shared with her college roommate and best friend. The house looked nothing like it had then. When she and Shannon had lived here together, it had been filled with comfortable, plush couches and chairs, fabrics of rich reds, purples, greens, and blues accented with gold and silver in earthy and celestial patterns, and alive with family photographs, the clutter of work, and a wide array of Celeste's artwork and crafts. Now it was empty but for a small dining table, her computer desk and chair, a small shelving unit with her favorite books and movies, and a couple accent pillows on the window bench. In her old room were a cheap flea market dresser and a mattress on the floor. No TV. If she wanted to watch movies, she played the DVDs on her iMac. In even greater contrast, there weren't many art supplies on the shelves or in the drawers of her desk, only the bare minimum she needed to fill orders through her Etsy store or to create the images she used for the book covers she designed for self-published authors. Glancing over the meager collection, she winced.

Anyone walking in the front door might assume she was just moving in, but she'd been back in the house a couple days shy of two months now. She should have brought some of the furniture and trappings from her husband's house, but she hadn't been able to go back, so she'd told her sister-in-law to do with it whatever she pleased—the house and everything in it. Everything had been Marc's, anyhow, picked and purchased by him to suit his tastes. The only things that were Celeste's were her cat, her clothes, her computer, and her art supplies, and Grandma Letty had been kind enough to rescue those from the house in the days following Marc's death. All her artwork was gone, too. She'd used it to open her Etsy store, and the speed at which every last piece had sold had been the one spark of hope in her bleak existence, and one she'd be relying on along with her freelance design work now that she'd quit her job with Liberty Bay Advertising.

It's been two months today, she reminded herself for the tenth time in as many minutes. *It's okay to feel hollow today.*

But what about every other day? What excuse did she have for them?

A plaintive yowling at the front door answered her. She opened it to let her cat in. He arched his back and rubbed against her legs. When she didn't immediately bend down to pet him, he put his paws on her knee, met her gaze with his bright blue eyes, and meowed again in a blatant demand for attention. His love kindled a glow of affection in her heart that burned away some of the gloom, and she slid her sunglasses to the top of her head, then leaned down to pick him up, snuggling him close and burying her fingers in his long, black fur. He head-butted her, purring loudly enough to make a semi jealous.

"Yeah, it's about time to bring you in for the night, isn't it, Bard," she murmured. "Don't want any assholes who think it's funny to torture black cats on Halloween to get hold of you, sweet boy."

She carried him to the window bench and settled him on her lap. Absently, she stroked him and stared out the window. Sundown changed the sky from the cornflower blue of day to the peach of dusk and was reflected by the Kingston harbor. She watched the ferry depart for Edmonds with its lights glimmering in the still evening and its hull slicing through the glassy waters. More than once, she'd sat in this very window glancing between that view and her sketchpad with her pencil flying over the paper as she tried to capture every detail. Tonight, she only followed the ferry until it vanished around the point, braced herself for the impending parade of monsters, witches, princesses, and superheroes, and hoped the only ghosts who came knocking were the kind made of bed sheets.

Bard meowed again and stood on his hind legs with his front paws on her collarbone to tuck his nose under her jaw. Dutifully, she massaged his neck the way he liked it best and was rewarded with more loud purring.

"Are you sure you're a cat?" she asked him. "Because you have the empathy of a golden retriever."

With a sigh, she stood and set Bard on the floor, then

headed into the kitchen to scrounge for dinner. First she opened a can of food for her cat; he deserved a special treat tonight. For herself, she decided to heat up the grilled chicken risotto left over from last night. Two seconds after she popped it into the microwave, the first knock sounded on the door. She reached for her bowl of candy only to realize the bags were still piled unopened on her counter. She yanked her biggest mixing bowl out of the cupboard below her, tore open the bags, and dumped their contents into the bowl, then hurried to the door just as the trick-or-treaters knocked again. She slipped her sunglasses back into place over her eyes at the last minute as she jerked the door open. There were three kids—a young princess, a younger pirate, and an older kid dressed as the cloaked, masked killer from *Scream*.

"Trick-or-treat!" they chorused.

"Smell my feet…" the pirate said.

"Dad said we're not to say that part," the older kid chided, his voice muffled by his mask.

"Oh, right. I forgot."

"Sorry about that," the older kid said. "Hey! You're Trinity from the *Matrix* movies!"

"Yeah. I'm surprised you figured it out." Celeste glanced down at her costume and caught herself smiling at the unexpected connection with another human being. "Aren't those movies a bit before your time?"

"Nah. My dad and I have watched them together so many times. I *love* those movies."

"Me, too."

She doled out the candy for the trio and wished them a happy and safe Halloween. As they turned to leave, she saw a flash of the *Scream* killer's fake knife—the kind with the clear plastic shell filled with rivulets of scarlet liquid to look like blood. She jerked back and closed the door as hastily as she could without slamming it and leaned against it, staring blindly at the ceiling. Her heart hammered against her ribs and she gulped air as her lungs suddenly forgot how to breathe. With a shriek, she ripped the sunglasses off her face and hurled them across the living room, flinching when they struck her computer desk and the lenses popped out.

On wobbly legs, she wandered into the kitchen, then sank to the floor with her back to the counter. Those silent, unfeeling tears trickled down her face as the nightmare of that night seized control of her mind again. How many times had she replayed it? Shouldn't she be *beginning* to recover from that trauma by now? Because she wasn't.

Bard pushed his way onto her lap, and the fluffy warmth of him was a tether to reality. She curled her fingers through his silky midnight fur and hunched over him, appreciative of his steadfast companionship.

Her cell phone rang, and she let out a gasp. Trembling, she reached up to the counter above her head, and her searching fingers found it right where she'd left it who knew how many hours ago. A glance at its screen brought a flood of relief. Shannon.

She accepted the call.

"Hi," she said breathlessly. "Have you guys made it yet?"

"Yep. We pulled in to Mom and Dad's this morning," Shannon replied. The joy tinting her words was a welcome balm. "We're all over at Bill and Mary Grangers' house now. They get way more trick-or-treaters than Mom and Dad do, and since we're only in Washington for a few days, we figured this would be a good way to spend the most time with everyone. I'm hoping you'd like to join us, too."

"I, uh…." A new wave of panic pounded through her at the mention of Bill Granger. Had he told Shannon? He'd promised he wouldn't until she'd had time to adjust to being a new mom, but he'd also said he wouldn't wait forever. She gripped the phone so tightly that her knuckles ached.

Breathe, Celeste. In. Out. In… and out….

If Bill had told Shannon about Marc, she wouldn't have wasted breath on idle chitchat.

"Celeste?" A note of concern wormed its way into Shannon's voice. "Are you all right?"

"I'm… f-f…." She tipped her head back, closed her eyes, and pinched her lips between her teeth, hating how her voice quivered with the lie she couldn't make herself tell. Her breath rushed in with another gulp and she held it as her sanity splintered again. How was there a fragment of her left whole enough to crack?

"Celeste?"

She let the breath out and shook her head. "No, I'm not all right."

"Oh, sweetie," Shannon crooned. "We'll be there in twenty."

Celeste started to tell her not to come, to enjoy her evening with her family, but the words refused to cooperate because, stubborn selflessness aside, she needed her friend right now. She wiped under her eyes and forced herself to smile. "See you soon," she murmured.

It took a couple minutes to get a grip on herself, and in that time, another knock came. She couldn't bring herself to answer it. When she was able to collect enough willpower to get off the floor, she took the candy bowl and set it outside her front door, then selected a soothing New Age playlist on her iMac, turned the volume up all the way, and retreated to the window bench to wait for Shannon to show up while Enya's enchanting voice filled the house. Bard, her ever faithful shadow, returned to her lap, and she focused her attention on him, ignoring the memories screaming at her.

Almost exactly twenty minutes later, Shannon stepped through the front door without knocking, immediately strode to Celeste, and wrapped both her and the cat in a hug. Celeste let out a ragged breath, then turned her gaze to the front door as Shannon's husband entered with their two-month-old son. Even though they'd been on the road all day yesterday and this morning, they'd still pulled together more elaborate and involved costumes than she had. They were a family of sleek lions, and rather than going with store-bought, baggy cover-all costumes, they'd selected fitted tan clothing and trimmed themselves with matching fake fur. Their makeup was flawless. The baby's costume was handmade and, from what Celeste could see of him, he was adorable.

"Why do I feel like I've suddenly fallen into *The Lion King*?" Celeste asked as lightly as she could manage.

"Perhaps because you have?" Shannon replied.

Shannon hadn't yet seen her with short hair, nor had she been back to this house since she'd moved out, but she made no comment about either. She noticed, though; the light frown that drew her brows together was evidence that she wanted to ask about both. Instead, she waved Ty over.

He leaned down to hug Celeste, then introduced her to his son, Jack, who was sound asleep in his father's arms and utterly precious.

"He's beautiful," Celeste sighed. Her eyes locked on his soft, angelic face as pain of a different kind tightened around her chest.

"Are you up for holding him?" Ty asked gently.

She wanted to so much that it hurt, but at the thought of doing so, the claws of cold self-loathing clenched, digging deeper. She shook her head and pinched her eyes closed as those frighteningly emotionless tears threatened again. "I'm sorry… I can't."

"Oh, honey," Shannon whispered. She scooted Celeste's legs over and sat on the bench with her. "What can we do?"

Celeste opened her eyes and stared out the window at the darkening twilight. A handful of stars had come out but nothing like the sparkling tapestry she remembered from her trip to Northstar last Christmas. Yearning blossomed like a rose of the most exquisite and ethereal amethyst hue—the rose of creativity, openness, and infinite possibility, all the things she desperately needed.

"Do you think I could find a place to rent in Northstar for a couple months?" Her lips twitched in a humorless smile as she recalled what she'd said to Shannon right here in this house almost three years ago. "I think it's my turn to have a good old fashioned *late*-twenties identity crisis."

"When are you thinking about coming out?"

"I thought I'd follow you guys home."

Ty frowned. "The Hammonds' cabin is booked until

March, but there are a couple cabins by the ski hill that the owners sometimes rent out if they don't plan to use them. We'll find something, and if you have to camp out on our couch for a little while until we do, so be it. You ladies talk about whatever you need to talk about, and I'll make a couple phone calls to see what I can find out."

Celeste flashed him an appreciative smile and watched him step into the kitchen to make his calls. "You found a good man, Shannon. And I know it doesn't show right now, but I am so happy for you."

"Yes, I did, though I think it's probably more accurate to say he found me. I might've gone the rest of my life without realizing what a special love we have. But back to you and this wild hair of yours. What about your job? That's pretty short notice, and will they give you any more time off? Or can you telecommute?"

"I quit my job. Today was my last day." Celeste hugged herself, trying to keep that memory at bay with all the rest determined to swamp her. "Turned in my resignation two weeks ago."

"What are you going to do for money?"

She saw the intent in Shannon's eyes and cut her off before her friend could open her mouth to voice it. "Don't you dare offer to lend me money. I have to do this myself."

"You don't have to. We're here for you, Celeste, however you need us."

"I know that, and believe me, I need you. But I need to…." She stumbled on the admission that she needed to start fresh standing on her own or she'd never be able to escape the memories of her life with Marc. "I can take care of myself."

"I'm well aware of that. You've always been one of the most independent people I know. But *how* are you going to take care of yourself? I'm asking so I know where you might let me help you."

"I have my Etsy store and my freelance design business. They're both doing pretty well. Things will be tight until I can build up my client base a bit more, and I might have to let go of this place and move in with Grandma Letty when I come back until I can find a new place to live, but if I can find a cheap enough place in Northstar, maybe I'll be able to keep it. Either way, I'll be fine."

"May I ask why you quit your job at Liberty Bay Advertising? You love that job."

"I did. But I blew up at my assistant two weeks ago. Over *nothing*. If that had been the first outburst, I would've stayed, but everything just…. I couldn't handle it anymore."

Confusion pinched Shannon's brows together.

Celeste sighed. She'd managed to keep her secret from her best friend for Shannon's sake, but she couldn't do it anymore. "I lied to you, Shannon. About Marc." She drew a deep breath. "Everything about him and our marriage."

"Good news," Ty interrupted. When he noticed their serious expressions, he held up his free hand. "Sorry. I can wait my turn."

"That's okay," Celeste told him. "What's the good news? I could use some."

"Dad says one of those cabins by the ski hill will be available to rent by next weekend. It's an A-frame with a great view of the mountains, an open floor plan downstairs, and a loft for sleeping. And it's cheap—just a couple hundred a month. You'll have to pay for electricity, your Internet and phone, and the propane, but it has a wood stove, so it won't cost much to heat."

"Sounds perfect. Thank you, Ty." She reached for his hand and Shannon's and gripped them tightly. "I was just telling Shannon how lucky she is to have you. And how lucky I am to have you both in my life."

"The feeling is mutual," he replied. He glanced around the house. "The cabin is furnished, but do you want to bring your things? We can rent a U-Haul and tow it over for you."

"Yeah, I think… I think that's what I'd like to do."

Then, if I decide I don't ever want to come back, all I'll have to do is tell my landlord.

That prospect merged with gratitude for her friends and saturated her, filling in all the fractures in her soul. For the moment, she didn't feel so shattered. "About Marc—I didn't want to tell you before because you'd *just* had Jack, but since I'm going to be foisting myself on you for the next couple months, it's time I told you both the truth. All of it."

* * *

Trouble.

That's the word that sprang to Brodie's mind when the svelte beauty strode out of the pool house in a simple but oh-so-sexy one-piece, one-shoulder black swimsuit. Slender and toned with proud shoulders and the kind of feminine curves that made it impossible not to stare, she was breathtaking. He watched her step cautiously behind Ty and Shannon Evans around the ice-crusted boardwalk to the Ramshorn Hot Springs' larger pool. With a body like that swathed in black—glossy sable hair cropped to chin length, shiny black polish on short, no-nonsense nails, and dark, defiant eyes in addition to the black swimsuit—she exuded a don't-fuck-with-me confidence, and Brodie had a strong suspicion he'd end up ignoring that warning.

She was trouble, all right. Trouble wrapped around a maimed core, and he'd never had much luck leaving wounded animals alone to suffer.

"Jesus, Brodie," his sister muttered, "you stare any harder and your eyes'll fall right outa your head."

"Let 'em fall out."

Ainsley narrowed her blue eyes and studied the newcomer. "You think that's your new neighbor?"

"Seeing as she's here with Ty and Shannon, I'd say most likely so, sprite."

"Ooo, boy. This'll be fun to watch."

"Uh-huh." He moved closer to the stairs as Ty and the women dropped their towels on the bench that ran the length of the pool. He snorted. *Leave a wounded animal alone? Yeah, right. They're goddamned magnets to me.*

"Gallus," Ainsley uttered under her breath.

He didn't know if she was calling him or Shannon's companion reckless. If the latter, she was probably right; the stew of anger and pain simmering in the woman's eyes— rich brown, he saw now that she was close enough— certainly gave the impression of rashness. If Ainsley referred to his impulse to investigate that concoction, she was *definitely* right.

The two women descended the stairs and slipped into the water while Ty walked down to the deep end and dove in. Shannon and her friend lingered on the steps.

"Evening, Shannon. When did you get back from

Washington?" Brodie asked in greeting. "And where's Jack?"

"Oh, hi, Brodie, Ainsley. I didn't see you there," Shannon replied.

She waded over, but her companion remained on the steps with water only up to her lower ribs. For a moment, she watched them with a faint frown. Then she propped her elbows on her thighs and leaned over her legs with her face tilted to the stars, and the sorrow that washed over her face made Brodie's heart ache.

"We just got home a couple hours ago, and Jack is currently being spoiled by Grandma Phoebe and Grandpa Hunter," Shannon said when she reached Brodie and his sister.

"I'm sure they missed him," he remarked.

She nodded with a laugh. "They all but kidnapped him the second we walked in the door, so we decided to take some time for ourselves."

Ty surfaced a few feet away and greeted Brodie and Ainsley before pulling his wife into his arms. "How's it going? Think you guys'll be able to open the ski hill a little early this year?"

"It's looking that way."

"No Brendan tonight, so I guess you already took him up to his mom's."

"Yeah, right after school. There's some movie opening tonight in Butte he wants to see. So, Shannon, who's your friend?" Brodie inclined his head toward the onyx-haired woman.

"Allow me to introduce you properly," Shannon said, waving her friend over.

The woman pushed off the stairs and glided through the water over to them. When she regained her feet beside Shannon, the sadness he'd seen had vanished. She was a few inches shorter than her auburn-haired friend, he noted— petite but definitely not dainty. And heaven help him, with water droplets and rivulets shimmering on her skin, she was even more stunning.

"Brodie, this is my best friend and former roommate, Celeste Dawson. She'll be your neighbor for the next couple months. Celeste, this is Brodie Dunn and his sister, Ainsley. They and their parents own the Northstar Ski Hill, so these two would be the ones to talk to about getting your board and skis waxed."

Not shy, either, he mused as she brazenly looked him over with her lips pursed ever so slightly and her eyes narrowed in appreciation. *Jings, crivens, an' help ma boab.*

"Good to meet you both."

In contrast to Shannon's clear, musical voice, Celeste's voice was a touch throaty and induced a curious wave of tingles. She extended her hand first to Ainsley and then to Brodie. Firm grip but brief, and when she pulled her hand back, she folded her arms. Defensive. She continued her perusal, however, and he sensed an undercurrent of a to-hell-with-it temper. Reckless, he thought again, or *gallus* as his Scottish-born father would say.

"You ski?" Ainsley asked before Brodie could recover his wits enough to form a proper response.

"Ski, snowboard, cross-country ski, and snowshoe. And none of it as often as I'd like."

Yeah, you're in trouble, lad. Brodie grinned. "You'll have ample opportunity here."

"I'm counting on it. What's this about the ski hill possibly opening early this year?"

"We've had an unusually snowy fall so far, and we've already got a good base piling up. We may even be able to open before Thanksgiving, and that hasn't happened in the years we've owned it."

"Lucky me."

"Have you seen your cabin yet?"

"Just the outside. Ty and Shannon took me up to it right after we landed in Northstar. That road is pretty steep, and I'm not sure my little two-wheel drive car will be able to handle it if it snows too much. They weren't sure if it's plowed."

"Only by yours truly. Even so, it can still be snotty."

"Why don't you park your car down at the ranch," Ty suggested, "and use one of our trucks while you're here?"

Celeste's brows dipped into a scowl, but it was gone in a flash, replaced by a flicker of despair. "Ty, I—"

"You can and you will," Shannon interrupted. "Because you're practical and you know one of the trucks would be a lot safer to drive."

Celeste snapped her mouth closed and pressed her mouth into a thin line, visibly suppressing whatever annoyance or anxiety gripped her. "Sorry," she whispered. Then she affected a too-bright smile that was clearly forced. "That'd be great. Thank you."

Brodie glanced between the two women, noting the concern evident in Shannon's eyes and the wincing regret in Celeste's. He suspected Celeste was fiercely independent, and the fact that she had yielded and accepted assistance made him believe something bad had happened to her, and it had backed her into the untenable position of needing help. Just like when he came across an animal needing help, his mind immediately started working out the logistics of how he could give her a hand without provoking her pride.

"It's probably presumptuous of me to say you'll like the A-frame," he said, pushing aside his natural inclination to scoop her into his arms and hold her until that defiant hopelessness left her eyes, "but I think you will. I wanted to buy it when I bought my place, but the owner wouldn't sell. Very cozy and airy with that open floor plan downstairs."

"From what Ty's told me, I'd say you're right. He says it has a great view of the mountains with big windows and a lot of light. That'll be great for my work."

"You're not here on an extended vacation?"

"Well, I am, but I'm fortunate to be able to work from anywhere I can set up my computer and work space."

The catch in her voice was curious, but Brodie figured now wasn't the time to ask her what the downside of her arrangement was. "What do you do for work?"

"Freelance design and a few paintings, jewelry, and whatnot I sell on Etsy. What about you? I know you work at your family's ski hill, but that's only a seasonal gig, isn't it?"

"I ramrod a construction crew for a contractor in Devyn in the spring, summer, and early fall."

She eyed him again, lingering on his face and shook her head. "You're not the ramrodding type."

"You caught me. But I do run the crew."

"What do you build?"

"Residential mostly. Houses, barns, sheds, shops.

That sort of thing."

"Shall the rest of us leave you two alone to chat?" Ainsley inquired. She glanced between him and Celeste with copper brows lifted.

"If you're offering," Brodie quipped, "be gone, wee lass."

Ainsley splashed him, nailing him right in the face with a wall of water. Then, with a smug gleam in her eyes, she kissed his cheek. Grinning, he sluiced the water from his face and rubbed it out of his eyes as his sister bid everyone good night and headed for the changing rooms inside the pool house.

"Wee lass? What are you, Scottish?" Celeste asked.

"Half plus a few drops from Mum's side. Dad's family has raised sheep and cattle on the same croft above the cliffs near Durness in northwest Scotland for generations. We hop the pond to visit the family over there every other year. When we don't go there, they come here."

"With that classic Scottish red hair, I should've guessed." A faint smile brightened her face. She glanced toward the pool house. "Your sister is beautiful. She has such delicate features, and I love her freckles. They make her look so elfin, like a sprite straight out of an enchanted forest. And you're not so bad yourself."

"Thanks. Ainsley *is* beautiful. She's also a pain in the arse sometimes," he said. How curious that Celeste should use the exact term he'd called his sister by most of Ainsley's life. "You have any siblings?"

"No."

"Lucky you."

"Maybe. Maybe not."

He liked the way she held his gaze when she said that, calling him out on his lie. He chuckled. "Caught me again. She *is* a pest at times, but even when she is, I still love her. I'd give my own life to keep her safe and happy."

"I bet you would."

That gentle assertion so sharply contrasted the audaciousness that he leaned back with brows raised. This girl had more layers than a bristlecone pine had rings, and he was suddenly keen to peel them back. But not tonight. Not for a while yet, he deduced.

Glancing around the pool, he realized that Ty and Shannon had sequestered themselves over by the pipe gushing hot water straight from the spring into the pool. "I'd best let you get back to your friends. It's getting late and I need to get home to feed my critters."

"It was good to meet you." The sudden warmth in her eyes surprised him and lent a genuineness to her words that told him she wasn't merely being polite. Then it was gone, and when she spoke again, her voice held a potent and sultry entreaty. "Don't be a stranger, Brodie. We *will* be neighbors for a while, after all."

That was another idea he wasn't going to investigate tonight. Smiling, he said, "Stop by the ski hill any time with your skis and board, and we'll get 'em waxed for you. See you soon, Celeste."

Ainsley was already waiting in his truck by the time he walked out of the pool house again fully dressed with his swim trunks rolled in his towel. He tossed his wet swim gear in the bed of his truck. As cold as it was tonight, they'd undoubtedly be frozen by the time he dropped Ainsley off at her cabin at the foot of the road up to his. That's what a dryer was for, though, right?

It wasn't until he'd started his truck and backed out of the parking spot that he noticed her sad, contemplative expression as she stared at the stars.

"What's wrong, sprite?" he asked softly.

"It's been almost thirteen years," she murmured, "and I can barely remember her anymore."

He didn't have to ask for clarification; he knew exactly what she was thinking about. This time of year, it was a topic never far from her mind or his or their mother's. "Well, you *were* only twelve. It's been more than half your life since she died."

"You still remember her pretty clearly, don't you? You were eighteen, and you were a lot closer to her than I was."

"The edges are beginning to dull now," he admitted. "But she'll never fade away completely because we won't let her. Any particular reason why you're thinking about her tonight?"

"Shannon's friend, Celeste."

"What about her?"

"Do you think maybe Inez is trying to tell you something? I mean, you have this giant soft spot for wounded things, and here comes this woman who's obviously been hurt worse than any animal you've taken in… and her name is Celeste."

A heavenly name, for sure. And it was under a starry sky like this the night before Inez died that she'd made him promise to never let a hurting creature suffer alone. *As if I could.*

"You follow me?" Ainsley asked.

"I follow you," he murmured, "but people aren't like animals, Ains. I can't fix her simply by offering her a warm home and kind words."

"Can't you? Seems to me like that's exactly what she needs."

He glanced sideways at her. "Didn't you just call me gallus not half an hour ago for thinking like that?"

"Yeah, but…." She tucked her legs against her chest and folded her arms around them. "Did you see her face when she was sitting on the steps by herself before Shannon introduced her? She looked so lost."

"I saw. I'd bet the ski hill that's exactly why she's here."

He also recalled the woman's blatant appraisal of him and the solicitous way she'd told him *don't be a stranger*, but he didn't bring that up, certain his voice would reveal how the idea of taking her up on that offer made his heart pound. *Layers*, he thought again. *Lots of 'em.*

As he turned onto Lightning Ridge Road at the base of the ski hill and pulled up in front of Ainsley's cabin, he reached over and gripped her shoulder with his hand in as much of a hug as he could manage with her sitting across the cab. A sprite straight from an enchanted wood, Celeste had called Ainsley. She'd nailed it. And like the pure-hearted sprite she was, Ainsley couldn't stand to see anyone in pain any more than he could. It gave her an innocence that, at times like this, made her seem a lot younger than twenty-five.

"Good night, sprite," he murmured. "Stars guard your dreams."

She took his hand and squeezed. "And yours. See ya

tomorrow."

He waited until she was inside the cabin before he headed up the road toward home. Lightning Ridge Road turned sharply just past Ainsley's house, then climbed up the side of the ridge that jutted out from the southeast flank of the ski hill. As the road crested the ridge, it broke out of the trees onto a flat opening with a breathtaking view of the eastern Northstar Mountains currently awash in the light of a waxing gibbous moon. His cabin sat just beyond the tree line down a sixty-foot driveway. The road curved back toward the western ridges, ending another tenth of a mile above his house at the A-frame Celeste would be renting for the next two months. He could see her temporary home from his front door, dark tonight but with its windows reflecting the moon. It would be nice to see light glowing from within and smoke curling from the chimney again.

That's what I can do for her.

The owner of the A-frame, a single, older gentleman from back East, had been out for a couple weeks in late October and had had the propane tank filled before he'd left for home but hadn't had time to restock the firewood. Brodie still hadn't unloaded his firewood trailer from last weekend, so it'd be no trouble to haul it up there tomorrow when Celeste moved in.

Satisfied with that plan, he climbed out of his truck and headed into his cabin. Two bouncy Labrador retrievers and a pair of yowling cats greeted him. He kicked the door closed behind him and reached down to pet each in turn. Even with them here to greet him so enthusiastically, the house felt empty without Brendan. It did every weekend when the boy was with his mother in Butte, and though he'd encouraged the arrangement, Brodie still missed the little bugger.

Sensing the dip in his mood, Jake, the yellow lab, whined. His foster sister, the black lab, Charlie, cocked her head and wagged her tail.

"I know you miss him, too."

The two cats—the white, tailless Moon and the black Binx—bumped against his legs, meowing. "And you two. You're just hungry, aren't you? You couldn't care less about Brendan or me as long as your food bowl is full."

He let the dogs out to do their business while he prepared dinner for the critters. Once they were all back in, fed, and adequately acknowledged with pets, Brodie wandered into the living room to the front window to admire the view. He wondered if Celeste liked animals. He hoped so, because not liking animals was a deal breaker for him. It never ceased to amaze him the unconditional love given by even an abused dog like Charlie, an abandoned Christmas puppy like Jake, a homeless stray like Binx or a tortured cat like Moon, whose tail had been so cruelly mangled after she'd been tied to a stake by it that it had needed to be amputated. It was so pure and so healing, that love, and he would never understand how people could take it and throw it away… or worse, crush it. If he taught his son nothing more than to treat animals with the same love they gave, he'd consider himself a success as a father because that compassion would carry over into the rest of his life. It might not make him a rich man, but it would make him a good one, and Brodie couldn't ask for anything more than that.

His mind drifted back to Celeste, something he had

a feeling it would be doing a lot over the duration of her stay in Northstar. From what he'd gathered about her tonight, she wasn't much different than his rescues—wary and unsure of herself with her confidence shaken. Had someone taken her love and crushed it or cast it aside? She was just as wary as Charlie, Moon, and Binx had been at first.

With his hands in his pockets, he stood at the front window and lifted his gaze to the glittering night sky, thinking back on his conversation with his sister. Celeste. A name inspired by the beauty of the heavens. He could almost see the watchful gaze of his half-sister in the stars.

"What are you trying to tell me, Inez?"

Two

CELESTE TURNED THE KEY in the lock and pushed the front door open. Or rather, the back door. It opened into a mudroom with a washer and dryer on the left wall. A tool bench on the right. Against the interior wall was a built-in bench for taking shoes off with coat hooks and shelves above and cubbyholes for shoes below. The door straight ahead from the outer one led into the kitchen, which was surprisingly spacious and laid out efficiently. As she stepped further into the A-frame, she noted three stools on the living room side of the island. The stairs to the loft, which covered the back half of the cabin, were to her immediate left with their base in the main living area; there was ample storage under them. A small dining table with four chairs sat to the left side of the living area, and a single couch faced the big windows at the front of the cabin. There was a nook in the southern wall with a small window that would be the perfect place to set up her computer desk and work area. A newer wood stove with a built-in fan sat in the front left corner, and a door in the center of the front wall opened onto a deck with a short flight of stairs down to the front yard. She thought she spied a stone fire pit under the snow in the middle of the yard. Four log benches sat around it in a circle. She was definitely going to have to see about buying some firewood now, or borrowing a chainsaw to cut her own. Maybe there was one in the shed out back.

All in all, the A-frame perfectly fit her idea of a cozy Montana cabin with all-wood walls and a pine floor covered in durable moose-and-bear-themed rugs. Aside from the north-woods-style fixtures that looked like they'd come straight out of a Cabela's catalogue, there were very few decorations. No pictures or paintings, no knickknacks, and not much else in the way of personal touches. The urge to rectify that was potent and unexpected. After two months of living in a bare house alone, why should this cabin with its functional if dated furniture that at least gave the impression of a long habitation inspire her to leave her mark on the space? *Because it's new and there's nothing of Marc here, no memory of him to taint it.*

Even the house she'd shared with Shannon had more than a few memories of him; nervously waiting for him to pick her up for their first date, the first time they'd made love, and his impromptu proposal right there on the front steps with a fiery sunset behind him.

"I take it the owner doesn't use this place much," she said, abruptly slamming the door on those memories.

"Couple weeks a year during hunting season is about

all," Ty replied.

"Pity. It's a lovely place." She walked over to the front windows and yanked the heavy green curtains open. A brilliant flare of awe ignited in the shadows of her heart, and she inhaled sharply. "Oh, you weren't joking about the view, Ty. It's spectacular."

"Isn't it? It almost makes me jealous."

"Don't know why. The one from your place is pretty great, too."

Ty handed his son to Shannon, then gestured to the back door. "Shall we get this done?"

"If you want, you can just drop the trailer and I can unload it myself. I know you need to get back to the ranch to meet your new client."

"I have time to help."

Between the two of them—Shannon had her hands full with Jack—they had the trailer unloaded and her few pieces of furniture moved into place in less than half an hour. Celeste would unpack the boxes later; she didn't need help with that. Even with the cabin fully furnished by the owner, the place didn't look remotely cluttered with her additional belongings. Since the house came with a dining set larger than her own, she set her table near her desk to use as an additional work surface. The single chair she stood beside the front door for a place to sit and put her boots on or take them off so she wouldn't have to tromp through or around the house to the mudroom.

Finally, Celeste brought Bard in. He let out a yowl to let her know he wasn't pleased she'd left him in the truck she'd be borrowing from Ty and Shannon, so she apologized and set his crate in the middle of the living room floor, then opened the door. In a most un-cat-like fashion, he boldly strutted out of the carrier, gave Celeste's knee his ritualistic head-butt, and made his way around the room, nosing everything for a few minutes and peering into the nooks and crannies before promptly flopping in front of the cold wood stove, unbothered by his new surroundings.

"I swear he's a dog trapped in a cat's body," Shannon mused.

Celeste laughed softly and squatted beside her cat to stroke her hand from his head all the way to the tip of his tail. He responded with his usual loud purr. "He's a character, and I don't know if optimism is a trait within the feline spectrum of emotion, but I'd say it's in his. It's like he trusts that everything will work out, so he doesn't sweat anything. Not even a seven-hundred-mile car ride to a strange new house."

"You found a special boy, Celeste."

"Yes, I did."

After a moment, Bard got up again and wandered over to Ty. Sitting at the man's feet, he regarded Shannon's husband with luminous blue eyes narrowed. Then he meowed plaintively, and Ty dropped to a knee to obey the blunt demand for attention.

"I knew you were a horse whisperer, but I didn't know you were a cat whisperer, too," Celeste remarked. "He typically doesn't like men."

"Cat whisperer. Funny. Now that we've got you all moved in," Ty said, still petting the cat, "I need to head out. Want me to bring in that box from your SUV, Shy Eyes?"

Shannon nodded. "Thanks, love."

"What box?" Celeste asked, eying her friends.

Ty grinned and scooted out the door.

"We got you a house-warming gift," Shannon replied.

"Shannon, you guys have already done too much for me."

"It's nothing much, I promise. I just noticed that you didn't have much for paints and canvases, so we remedied that. I'd like to see some of your artwork on the walls again because our old house was *way* too bare."

Celeste agreed but she didn't say *why* she hadn't put any of her artwork on display or that she wasn't likely to hang it here, either. As soon as she thought that, she chastised herself. She was here in Northstar precisely to put that emptiness behind her, to reconnect with her soul, and to reengage her zeal for life.

Fall seven times. Stand up eight.

With her cat once again sprawled in front of the wood stove and eying her as if to ask where his fire was, Celeste turned to Shannon. "You have to stop helping me. I need to—"

"I heard you the first time on Halloween," her friend replied sharply. "I get that you need to prove to yourself that you're strong enough to overcome this, Celeste. I do. But you've been trying to work through this on your own for long enough, and leaning on the people who love you isn't weakness."

"I know it—"

Ty nudged the door open with his hip, and Celeste snapped her mouth closed to watch him carry an awkwardly large box inside. Then she scowled at Shannon. Her friend met her anger without flinching.

"Here you go." Ty set the box on the table by her desk, then turned to embrace her. If he noticed the tension in her body, he gave no sign, but since it was part of his job to sense the tiniest shifts in mood from the horses he trained, she was certain he'd marked it. "Welcome, officially, to Northstar."

"Thank you, Ty," she replied curtly.

"My pleasure. We're here for you, Celeste." His tone was pure gentleness and understanding, and despite her stubborn pride, it made her tremble with gratitude. "I wish you would've let us be there for you from the beginning, but I get it, so I hope a couple months here will help you find the peace you need. God knows there aren't too many places more peaceful than Northstar."

When Celeste's lips lifted, the smile was genuine. "That's for sure."

He hugged her again, then kissed his wife and his son. "See you ladies later."

Celeste walked over to the windows and let her eyes wander over the incredible vista, not really seeing the white and gray landscape or the flurry of snowflakes drizzling from the sullen sky. She loved days like this that evoked daydreams of an exhilarating plunge down a steep slope with the fresh powder hissing beneath her snowboard or a long, brisk trek through snowy woods on cross-country skis. Or she *used* to. Just like she used to love painting for the sheer joy of watching some beautiful scene take shape on the canvas. There were a lot of things she'd loved before the trauma of Marc's death had encased her in a coffin of numbness. But that's why she was here—to get away from the deluge of memories with the hope that, without them constantly assaulting her, she might again find the joy in her favorite activities.

"I'm guessing Marc's the reason Bard doesn't care much for men," Shannon remarked, drawing Celeste out of her dark ponderings.

"You'd have to ask him," Celeste replied, "but I'd say that's a safe assumption to make."

"I still can't believe you didn't tell me." Shannon's expression turned mournful. "What's more, I can't believe *Bill* didn't tell me."

"I begged him not to. Shannon, you and Ty were *brand new* parents, and I couldn't—"

"I appreciate you not wanting to spoil our memories of that, but you're my best friend, and it kills me to know that you wouldn't let me help you through this."

"You're a great friend, Shannon, so don't—"

"How am I a great friend if I wasn't there for you when you most needed me?"

"Would you *stop* interrupting me?" Celeste snapped. "This isn't about you being a good friend or not, or about you needing to fix me. This is about me being so emotionally fucked up that I couldn't handle bringing *you* pain."

She wandered over to the couch and perched on the edge of the seat, hugging herself. Shannon sat beside her, cradling her sleeping son in her arms. Celeste didn't look at them. Couldn't.

"Before Marc died and after, your excitement over your pregnancy and the birth of your son and all the success you've had in your career.... It was something for me to hold on to—a source of hope that there might still be good things to come for me. If I told you the truth about what happened, it might dim that, and I needed every vibrant color of that rainbow. Because my world was colorless."

A knock sounded on the inside door, cutting off whatever response Shannon might've made.

Celeste frowned, glancing over her shoulder. "Who…?"

"C'mon in," Shannon called. "Door's open."

Shannon's brother and his family or their friends the Conners, Ty's parents or sister and brother-in-law—she figured her unexpected visitor might be any of them, perhaps dropping by to welcome her to the valley. But none of them stepped through the door as it opened. Instead, Brodie Dunn walked in grinning that roguish smile of his and looking like a lumberjack in a green plaid wool shirt and fitted blue jeans that showed off muscular legs. Her pulse accelerated as she took in the lines of him. With red hair, the beginnings of a beard, blue eyes prone to mirth, and a face that was both devilishly masculine and boyishly adorable, he wasn't the standard definition of sexy, but he certainly exuded sex appeal with broad shoulders, narrow waist and hips, and a thick-boned, sturdy build. Attractive but approachable. No, more than approachable. Inviting.

Celeste stood. Somewhere in the back of her mind, she figured she should at least welcome him to her home, but her manners took a back seat to her appreciation of the man himself.

"Brodie, hi," Shannon greeted, shifting her son to one arm and rising to embrace him as he strode into the living room. "What brings you by?"

"I come bearing a housewarming gift," Brodie said.

"For the love of all things holy, do I have 'charity case' tattooed to my forehead?" Celeste whirled on Shannon. "What did you do? Invite half of Northstar to welcome me to the community?"

"Nope," Brodie replied. "This is all me."

"I'm going to try really hard not to be hurt by that," Shannon said in a careful, level tone, "because I know this isn't you. But I hope there's still enough of the Celeste I know and love left in you that you'll see how monumentally rude that was."

Celeste jerked back. It wasn't her friend's terse reprimand that shocked her. It was the need for it. "I'm sorry, Shannon. You're right." Turning to Brodie, she said, "That *was* rude of me, and I apologize. I'm a little tense these days, and even under better circumstances, I've never been comfortable with accepting unsolicited assistance."

"So I gathered." He flashed her a grin. "And that was quite a mouthful. A simple 'my bad' would've sufficed."

Damn, he's quick. To her immense astonishment, she returned his smile and it wasn't forced. She glanced over him again, finding more to like the longer she looked. "It's very kind of you to think of me. I hope you didn't go out of your way to do so."

"Why don't you come outside and decide for yourself?"

Outside? Celeste nearly groaned but followed him and Shannon out to the driveway. Her mouth fell open. Attached to the shiny new dark blue pickup she presumed was his was a rusty old truck bed that had been converted into a trailer. It was loaded with firewood. She was at once overwhelmed by his thoughtfulness and irritated that she was going to be indebted to him and Shannon and Ty and who knew how many others for their generosity. Why couldn't they all just leave her alone to fight her way out of this mess like she needed to?

"I can't accept this, Brodie."

"Sure you can. I have enough wood to get me through the winter. This was extra Dad and I cut a few days ago just in case. I haven't gotten around to unloading it, and since old Fred's shed is empty, I figured I might as well bring it up. It's no big deal, I promise."

"Promise all you want, but it *is* a big deal. I was wondering not twenty minutes ago where I was going to get firewood this time of year, so thank you."

"My pleasure. If you want, I can split some for you and get you a good pile of kindling going after I get this unloaded and stacked. Just to get you started."

"I can handle the splitting and stacking myself, but thanks." As soon as the words left her lips, she wished she could take them back. Brodie was an attractive man who had a peculiar and intriguing effect on her, and spending some time with him might be good for her. Impulsively, she reversed her habitual dismissal. "On second thought, I may take you up on your offer. But I should probably find out first if you have a wife or girlfriend. Wouldn't want to get you in trouble with the missus."

"No wife, and no girlfriend at the moment, either, though I'm not sure how helping a neighbor would get me in trouble with her if I did. I'd hope any woman of mine would appreciate my… generosity…."

His voice trailed off when he met her gaze, and his pupils dilated as he caught her meaning. From the corner of her vision, Celeste saw Shannon's eyes widen. Later, she'd probably be horrified by her brazenness, but right now, she couldn't summon the energy to give a damn about the recklessness of propositioning a man she'd only met last night. He made her feel *something*. Exactly what, she couldn't yet tell, but she wanted to hold on to that feeling for as long as she could, exhausted by the endless emptiness and longing for even the tiniest glow of any sensation other than the brief flashes of anger or despair.

"How about we get your firewood unloaded and save the splitting for another day?" Brodie suggested.

"Probably a good idea," Shannon replied.

The spark of spirit winked out, and Celeste ground her teeth in annoyance. She pointed to the ground in front of the empty woodshed. "Just help me pile it over there, if you wouldn't mind, Brodie. I'll stack it later."

She climbed onto the top of the stack in the trailer with Brodie, and together, they tossed blocks into a pile in front of the woodshed. She tried not to let the fluid rhythm of his body distract her, but as she worked alongside him, it was impossible not to notice. She settled for a few covert glances. More than once, he caught her watching and smiled, unbothered and maybe even flattered. That addictive *something* tickled her again, and she latched on to it hungrily.

"You've done this before," he observed.

"A time or two." She continued tossing logs onto the pile without breaking her rhythm. She spent so much of her time sitting for her work that the manual labor felt good, and the tiny spark grew into a tiny flame. "I cut and split all my Grandma Letty's firewood. She has a wood stove in her house."

"What, you even know how to run a chainsaw?"

She nodded.

"Good on you, lass."

"Lass." She laughed softly. "I like that."

Too soon, they finished unloading the trailer, and Celeste jumped down to survey the pile of logs with her hands in her pockets. It had to be a full cord of wood, and it would save her a lot of money in heating costs. Money she could either save or spend on things that had once made her happy. Suddenly, the idea of curling up on the couch with her sketchbook in hand while flames writhed behind the glass in the door of the wood stove pranced into her mind, shedding light on another piece of herself that had been scattered beyond sight and reach for months, and right then, she wanted nothing more than to be alone to make that image a reality.

Almost as if he'd sensed the direction of her thoughts, Brodie met her gaze again with a mischievous, lopsided grin that told her plainly he hadn't forgotten about her earlier intimation.

"Let me know if you want a hand stacking or splitting all that later." He gestured to the firewood. "But in the meantime, I'll let you get back to settling in."

Celeste watched him slide in behind the wheel of his truck, roll his window down, and lean out.

"Don't be a stranger, neighbor," he added with a wink before he turned the key in the ignition.

Shannon barely waited until his truck had crossed the property line before she turned to Celeste, gaping. "I cannot believe you. I'm not sure you could have said it more clearly if you'd come right out and asked him to sleep with you."

"Not everyone has a perfect life like you do," Celeste retorted. Immediately, she regretted it and let out a growl. "I'm sorry. Again. You deserve every bit of happiness you've found and then some."

"He really messed you up."

It wasn't a question, but Celeste nodded in confirmation anyhow.

"Do me a favor, will you?"

She gave Shannon a suspicious sideways glance and waited for her to finish.

"Go easy on Brodie, all right? He's a good guy, and he'd take whatever you threw at him without a word of complaint no matter how much it might hurt him."

That stung. Celeste folded her arms and narrowed her eyes defensively.

"Don't give me that look. You're suffering and lashing out at everyone who tries to help you because of it. And you know you are." Shannon wrapped her in a one-armed hug. "I'm going to head home because I get the feeling you need to be alone right now."

Celeste tried not to let her relief show but failed. "Thanks. For everything."

Shannon only nodded in acknowledgement and headed to her SUV. Celeste trudged to the door of her cabin, leaning against the doorjamb to watch her friend tuck her infant son into his car seat. She waved as Shannon drove away, then she turned toward the tool shed, hoping there would be an ax inside. She located one just inside the door and selected a larger log to use as a chopping block. When she had enough kindling to start a fire and enough wood split to see her through the night, she hauled it all inside and started a fire in the wood stove.

Much better.

She stood back and watched the flames devour the wood, smiling when Bard resumed his position in front of the fire with eyes closed in contentment.

Next, she went through the box of art supplies Shannon and Ty had bought her. There were several canvases and an assortment of oil, acrylic, and watercolor paints along with some pastels, conté sticks, charcoal, pencils, sketchpads, and watercolor paper. It shouldn't surprise her that Shannon knew her exact preferences as they'd lived together for much of their decade-long friendship, but she pressed her knuckles to her lips and blinked away the threat of tears. She was truly blessed to have such a thoughtful friend, and one of the first things she needed to work on was her half of that friendship.

She let her fingers skip over the collection of supplies and silently thanked Shannon. It might be a while before she broke them out, if she ever did, but it was nice to have them. Just in case.

After she unpacked all her work supplies and computer and set up her work station, she decided to save the rest of her settling in for later in favor of getting caught up on business—answering emails from current and prospective clients, making a list of orders to fill for her Etsy store, and scheduling the new projects. It was relaxing to focus on work; that was one area of her life she could control. And the way things were looking, she'd be able to splurge on a season ski pass to the Northstar Ski Hill by the time it opened even if it opened early as Brodie had said it might.

Brodie.

Her lips lifted again at the reminder of him. Glancing over her shoulder out the big front window on the dining room side of the living area, she could just see the peak of his roof down the hill. When she stood and walked to the windows, she could make out the rest of his house through the thickening curtain of snow. Not once in the two months since Marc's death had she so much as looked at another man… until she'd walked out of the Ramshorn's pool house last night and noticed Brodie watching her with such gratifyingly obvious appreciation. And she hadn't only *looked* at him. She'd all but invited him to hop into bed with her. The sudden and intense desire was delicious, and she decided she wouldn't chide herself for the spontaneity that inspired it.

Three

IT WAS GOOD TO BE WORKING at the ski hill again. Brodie enjoyed his construction job and helping with his parent's Scottish Highland cattle operation, but the ski hill was his passion. The air of unhurried enjoyment about it was a welcome change from the seriousness of building and ranching. People flocked to the slopes to have a good time, which meant they were usually in a good mood, and that jovial attitude infused the mountain with excitement and laughter. It didn't matter what task he was assigned to—running the lift, manning the grill at the lodge, instructing a group of eager first graders, or waxing boards and skis like he was at the moment—it never felt like work. That's what life was about, wasn't it? Living.

As short as her life had been, Inez had always known that, and he paused in his task to send her a silent thank you for teaching him.

He turned up the radio when a mid-tempo country song he liked came on, and he sang along as he worked, smiling as the beat of it and the lyrics thrummed through him. He was certain he didn't sound nearly as smooth or as seductive as the man serenading his new love and inviting her to have another dance with him, but as there wasn't anyone around to be bothered, who cared?

"Nice voice."

He jerked upright, banging his head on the low-hanging light over the worktable, and spun around to the front counter. Celeste stood on the other side of it with two snowboards in one hand and a pair of skis in the other. She regarded him with a sassy gleam in her brown eyes and one corner of her mouth lifted, and he couldn't help but smile back as he prodded the bump on his head.

"Thank ya, ma'am," he drawled, tipping his imaginary cowboy hat.

"Country fan, huh?" she inquired.

"You say that like it's a turn off."

"Not at all. I don't listen to it much, but I don't dislike it."

"Let me guess. You're a death metal kind of woman."

"Way off. Nineties and early two-thousands pop, new age, and movie scores."

"What, like the Backstreet Boys and Enya?"

"And the Spice Girls, Aqua, Enigma, and the *Braveheart* soundtrack, to name a few others. With a little electronic thrown in."

All music that suggested she had an upbeat, optimistic side, a firm grasp of herself, and a deep appreciation of the quiet moments in life. Layers, he thought again. And with each one he discovered, his curiosity doubled.

He let his gaze rake over her again, lingering when she didn't object to his appraisal. He usually preferred long hair, but that short style and the way it curved around her face and framed it was stunning on her. It let her eyes be the focus, and aside from the shadow in them, they were strikingly intelligent and compassionate. They reminded him of a doe—exactly the term Shannon had used more than once in describing her friend. That was about right. If Ainsley was a forest sprite, Celeste was a skittish doe, pure and wild and gracefully confident, but one that had been harshly wounded.

She was encased in black again, but the faux fur around her parka's hood was gray. Beneath the coat, he spied a coal-gray sweater. The lack of color was incongruous for someone who claimed to be an artist. Still, the dark monotony suited her, or rather, it suited the simmering anguish that clung to her like a fog and blurred the true beauty of her—the purity of spirit that flashed in her eyes now and again.

"*Braveheart*, eh? Well, now, there's something we have in common besides skiing. And speaking of skiing, what brings you to the hill, lass? Because I'm pretty sure you didn't come to compare our tastes in music."

"A little birdie told me you're the man to see about getting these waxed." She tapped her fingers against the snowboards and skis.

"The little birdie told you right."

"How much do you charge?"

"How's twenty bucks for your gear and ten for Shannon's sound?"

"Like a bargain." She tilted her head. "How'd you know the other board was Shannon's?"

"I'm psychic."

Celeste lifted a brow with amusement playing about her eyes and lips. "Uh-huh."

"She bought it from us just before she and Ty headed out to Washington." He chuckled. "I won't be able to get to them today. Is tomorrow morning soon enough?"

"As long as you aren't planning to open the hill tonight, tomorrow is perfect."

She leaned her equipment against the counter and pulled her wallet out of her coat pocket, then dug out thirty dollars and handed the cash to him. He rang up her sale, passed her the receipt, and added her board and skis to his log. Then he lifted the equipment over the counter, tagged them with her name and her friend's, and set them in the rack to the right of the worktable with the rest of the snowboards and skis he had to wax today.

"What time should I come by to pick them up?" Celeste inquired.

"I'll drop them by your cabin."

"Brodie, you don't have to do that."

He flashed her a grin. "I know I don't. I want to. And before you tell me off for helping you again, consider that maybe I'm not doing it because I think you're a charity case but because I simply enjoy doing nice things for people. I'm sure that's exactly why you just paid for Shannon's board, too."

Surprise briefly widened her eyes, but then it was

gone and she laughed softly, holding her hands up in a show of peace. "Well played, good sir."

This time, Brodie heard when the door to the ski shop opened, and he leaned over the counter to see who'd come in. He wasn't surprised to see Shannon with her son wrapped snuggly in her arms.

"Good morning, Brodie," she said brightly.

In sharp contrast to Celeste's colorless attire, Shannon was dressed in blue jeans, a wine-colored sweater, and a deep green parka, and Jack was swaddled in bright red and blue. She had her wallet out already and asked how much it would be to have her board waxed.

"Celeste already paid. I'll bring your board by the ranch tomorrow morning after I drop hers off."

She glanced sharply at her friend, then turned back to Brodie. "You're sweet. Thanks."

"Anything else I can do for you ladies?"

"Yeah," Celeste said. "Season passes. I'm not quite ready to buy one yet, and I don't even know if it'll save me any money, but I'll bet you can clear that up for me."

"Season pass is three-fifty," Brodie replied. "If you're planning to hit the slopes more than nine times while you're here, it'll save you money. But the price goes up Saturday to four-twenty-five, so you might want to decide quick."

"She'll be here enough to make even the four-twenty-five worth it," Shannon remarked.

Annoyance flickered across Celeste's face along with a touch of disappointment.

"I won't have the extra cash for a couple weeks," she murmured so quietly he figured she didn't mean to be heard.

"I'll get it for you," Shannon offered.

"No, you won't."

"You can pay me back."

"No, Shannon. I'll pay it myself straight up or I won't get it at all."

"You'd pay an extra seventy-five bucks just to assuage your pride?"

"Yeah, I would. And you ought to know why by now. I've repeated myself enough times."

"But it's okay for you to pay for my—"

"How about a job?" Brodie interrupted, his gaze trained on Celeste. "We could use an extra hand around here, and employees ski for free."

"I beg your pardon?" she blurted. Anger snapped in her eyes; her fight response had been triggered.

Again, he wondered what had backed this fawn-like nymph into a corner so that she no longer felt she could flee from uncomfortable situations, which was surely her natural inclination.

"Employees ski free," he said again, carefully enunciating. "And we're short staffed. You said you work from home as an artist, but if you could spare a few days a week to help around here, we could use someone of your considerable experience."

"Doing what?"

He grabbed her board and her skis and made a show of inspecting them. With that wear, she was a veteran boarder and skier. "Judging by these, I'd say whatever you want."

Her lips curved upward, but her eyes retained some of the cold fury. That to-hell-with-it attitude was firmly back in place. "You know, I think I might take you up on that.

Give me a couple days to see what my schedule looks like, and I'll get back to you."

Jack, who had been contentedly snuggled in his mother's arm, suddenly started crying—great gravelly shrieks—and Shannon hastily apologized, blushing. Celeste cringed.

"Ah, he's a sweet wee bairn," Brodie said gently. "Don't apologize, Shannon. Go do what you need to do."

She smiled gratefully and jogged out to her SUV. Brodie stared after her a moment with a wistful twist of his lips. He recognized that panicked embarrassment in her eyes and couldn't believe it had already been almost six years since he'd felt it himself. He missed the new joy of a baby and even that unbalancing belief that he had no idea what he was doing.

"How about we talk about this job over dinner tonight?" Celeste asked, her voice low and husky. "And if we feel like having a little fun afterwards…."

He shifted his gaze back to her. There was enough genuine interest in her bold inspection of him to make his heart race, but he sensed she was driven mostly by a need to retaliate and a desire for command when there was so much in her life beyond her control. Trouble. That's what she was, in every sense of the word that mattered to him. So, naturally, he had no hope of resisting.

"Now, that's a right tempting proposition," he replied thoughtfully. "But I'm a nice lad, and I don't believe in sex until after at least, oh, three dates."

"I don't believe you." She folded her arms on the counter and leaned forward, affecting a seductive simper. He didn't doubt her offer was authentic, but the manner in which she delivered it didn't fit her. "That's why you offered me a job, isn't it?"

"Nope. I offered because we're short-handed but also because I'd like to get to know you." He leaned casually against the counter, angling his body toward her. The way she pulled back a little confirmed that this brazen come-on was not her natural mode of operation. Still, there was a definite spark between them, and he wasn't about to let it fizzle; it had been too long since he'd felt anything like it. "Now, I'm not saying I'm not interested in sex, and if the job leads to it, who am I to turn down a beautiful woman?"

"So… dinner at my place tonight? I have a freshly stocked fridge and pantry, and I'm thinking a hearty Italian pasta dish sounds good."

"It sounds incredible, but unfortunately, I can't tonight. I have to head up to Butte to pick Brendan up from his mother's."

"Who's Brendan?"

"My son."

She lurched back, eyes wide. At once, the underlying innocence returned, again giving him the impression of a spooked doe. "You… have a son? H-how old is he?"

"He'll be six next month. I'd like to take a rain check on that dinner, if the offer's still on the table. Unless you have an issue with me having a kid."

She straightened and visibly reigned in her emotions. "Why would I have a problem with that?"

"Oh, I don't know, but the fact that that your eyes were about as big as saucers a second ago makes me think you might."

"I don't." She took a deep breath, flashed him a

smile. "Honestly. It just surprised me. Yesterday, when you said you didn't have a wife, I guess I didn't consider that you've *had* one."

"I haven't. So, how about that rain check, lass?"

"Rain check for dinner or sex?" She tried to bring back some of her earlier daring, but it was weak, overpowered by the sweetness that had infiltrated her eyes the moment she'd learned of his son.

"Just dinner. Like I said, I'm a nice lad," he replied softly. "This isn't you."

She met his gaze briefly in a moment of explicit vulnerability that zapped Brodie's heart like lightning, but before either of them could step through that open door, Shannon strolled in with her son in a much better mood. Celeste lowered her eyes, and he could almost hear the locks bolting as she closed the door again. When she lifted her gaze, she smiled.

"When should I stop by to officially apply for that job?"

"Has it been a day or two already?"

That brought a flicker of authenticity to her smile. "Seems there's not as much to think about as I thought."

"Dad'll be here Tuesday. He does all the hiring."

"See you then?"

"I'll make sure I'm here."

With a nod, Celeste told Shannon she'd be out in the car and strode out of the ski shop. Shannon turned to Brodie.

"I'm sorry about that."

"I already told you not to apologize for Jack. Been there, done that, Shannon, and it doesn't bother me a bit."

"Not for Jack," she replied. "For Celeste."

"What makes you think you need to apologize for her? Do I look offended or put out?"

"No. I just wish she'd let me help her. "

Brodie rested his hand on her shoulder and squeezed. "I don't think she's ready to be helped just yet."

Shannon regarded him with brows lifted skeptically. "Then why did she want to come out to Northstar for an extended visit?"

"She needs to breathe. She's where I was after Inez died—fighting against the unfairness and cruelty of life—and what she needs from you most is just to *know* that you're here for her when she needs you."

"Did she tell you…?"

"No, and I'm not going to ask you to tell me, either. I don't need to know yet, and if or when she's ready to tell it, I'd rather hear it from her, anyhow."

Shannon laughed softly. "Anyone ever tell you that you sound a *lot* like June Conner?"

"A time or two, and I'll take it as a compliment now like always."

She patted his hand, thanked him for his offer to bring her snowboard by the ranch the next morning, took her son, and left. Brodie blew out a breath and got back to work, again singing along with the radio. When he recalled Celeste's compliment of his voice, he smiled. She was fire and ice, that one, and he suspected she'd be a perfect temperature once the two sides tempered each other.

Thoughts of her occupied him all through the morning and afternoon and during the two-hour drive to Butte. As he navigated the narrow, icy roads of Walkerville that twisted, curved, and ended abruptly seemingly without reason, relief at the impending reunion with his son pushed Celeste aside though not out of his mind. He parked his truck in Stephanie's narrow driveway and stepped out into the crisp November night with his hands stuffed in his pockets to ward off the cold. Stephanie's house was perched at the very top of the hill that was Butte in the town of Walkerville, and the view from her front porch was phenomenal. Below him, the glittering lights of the conjoined cities stretched down the hill and across the valley almost to the foothills of the Highland Mountains.

Where else should a Highland lad settle but near the Highlands? his father had once replied when Brodie had asked why he'd chosen to settle in Southwest Montana.

Chuckling, Brodie turned toward the front door of his ex-girlfriend's house. He didn't get a chance to knock. The door popped open, and Brendan launched himself at Brodie, trusting his father to catch him without even a second to prepare. Used to Brendan's ritualistic greeting, Brodie caught him easily and lifted him in a bear hug.

"Papa!"

"Hi to you, too."

With arms still tight around his father's neck and legs gripping his waist, Brendan whispered, "Miss me?"

"Always," Brodie murmured.

It had only been two days since he'd seen his son, but he was as glad to see Brendan as he would be after weeks apart. For a moment, he tucked his face against Brendan's neck, reacquainting himself with the scent of him and the ever-growing weight of his small body. The restlessness that always plagued him when they were apart vanished, replaced by the relief of knowing with his own senses that his child was safe and whole and happy. Stephanie was a good if unwilling mother, and he trusted her wholeheartedly with their son, but a piece of him went missing when Brendan wasn't with him.

Out of habit, he braced an arm around his son's waist as he stepped inside, but Brendan didn't need any help holding on. Brodie pulled the door closed behind him with his free hand. The living room was vacant. "Steph?"

"Kitchen!"

Still carrying Brendan, he followed the sound of her voice to the kitchen in the back of the house. He found her and her boyfriend, Russ, mixing the ingredients for meatloaf, which explained why Brendan had been alone in the living room to see Brodie pull up. With half his brain still focused on Celeste, he couldn't help but compare the two women. Stephanie was taller but finer-boned with mousy features, medium brown hair, and eyes the color of sun-struck jade. She had a different kind of confidence, too—a relaxed, self-assuredness borne of a tragedy-free life filled with family and friends who loved her and laughed with her. In some ways, she was too much like him with her ease and willingness to make light of anything, and in other ways, they were too different, namely in her disinterest in parenthood and his keen desire for it.

She and Russ, though… they were a perfect match. Same sense of humor, same tastes in movies, music, and books, same disinclination to be parents, but also enough differences to keep things lively. Russ was a quintessential nerd and tech geek—narrow framed with the thin musculature of someone who spent very little time pursuing manual labor, dark blond hair, and amber eyes framed by sleek rectangular glasses with black frames. Brodie genuinely liked the man, and he was glad Stephanie had found him, because they were great together. She might've called it quits with Brodie just months after Brendan's birth, but he still cared about her, and seeing her happy made him happy, too.

"Zombie brains for dinner?" he inquired.

Laughing, Steph lifted her hands out in front of her and made a show of staggering toward him with hamburger and egg clinging to her fingers. "Brains… I want brains!"

Brendan squealed in fright, clinging tighter to Brodie. "Mom!"

"Hey, talk to your dad. He brought it up."

Brodie tilted his head back to study his son's face with a frown. "What's wrong, lad?"

"Steph and I were watching a zombie movie last night," Russ explained, "and Brendan crawled out of bed just in time to catch a scary part."

"Ah." Brodie smoothed Brendan's light brown hair back from his forehead. "Scared you, huh?"

The boy nodded, his blue eyes round.

"I know it looked real, but it's all just make believe—actors in makeup with digital effects."

"I don't want zombie brains for dinner," Brendan murmured. "Can we go get something else, Papa?"

"It isn't zombie brains. I was just teasing your mom. It's meatloaf, which I know you like because you always ask Nana and Granddad to make it for you."

"I just…." He eyed the bowl and chewed on his lips. "I don't want meatloaf tonight."

Brodie turned to Stephanie and offered her a sympathetic smile. "I know I said we'd stay for dinner, but would you mind if we didn't?"

"No, that's okay. I understand."

He nodded his head toward the front door in an invitation to walk out with them. She washed her hands, told Russ she'd be right back, and followed Brodie and Brendan out to his truck. After Brendan was buckled in, Brodie stepped out of the way so Stephanie could say goodbye.

"Love you, bud," he heard her say. "I really am sorry for the zombie thing. I hope I haven't ruined meatloaf for you forever now."

"It's okay, Mom. I love you, too."

Stephanie gave the boy a kiss on the cheek, then closed the truck door and faced Brodie. "I'm sorry about him waking up to a zombie movie. I tried to tell you I wasn't cut out to be a parent."

"And I still say bullshit. You're a good mom, Steph. That in there just now… that's something *every* parent deals with, even the best. Besides, I'm the one who brought up zombies."

"Yeah, but you're not the one he blamed." Her lips twisted in amusement. "Of course, you also wouldn't be watching a zombie movie after he went to bed, either."

"Nope." He shuddered. "I like my brains right where they are, thank you, and contemplating some undead thing trying to eat them is *not* something I enjoy."

"You know, for being such a big, strapping guy, you're kind of a sissy when it comes to scary movies."

"Kind of?" Brodie inquired with a brow lifted. "I'm

a damned coward."

She laughed and kissed his cheek. "Good night, Brodie."

"See you Friday."

Brodie climbed in behind the wheel of his truck and strapped himself in.

"Did you meet the new neighbor yet?" Brendan asked.

"Yes, I did."

"What's her name?"

"Celeste Dawson."

"Is she nice?"

"Yes, she is. But a little sad."

"How come?"

"I don't know yet."

"Is she pretty?"

"Very." Chuckling, Brodie started the truck and turned to his son, deciding to put an end to this game of twenty questions before Brendan got around to asking him if he wanted to marry Celeste. "Is Chicken Shack for the ride home going to be okay, or are you going to beg me to take you to Silverbow Pizza?"

"Chicken Shack is okay. I'm ready to go home."

"Didn't you have a good time with your mom and Russ? She said you guys went sledding up behind Tech."

"Yeah, we did. And I had a good time. I'm just ready to go home and pet Jake and Charlie and Moon and Binx."

"Ah, so it isn't *me* you missed," he teased. "You missed the dogs and cats."

"I missed them, too," Brendan admitted. He leaned over to hug Brodie's arm. "But I missed you most."

"What did I do to deserve such a wonderful kid as you?"

"Dunno, but I'm glad you're my papa."

"Me, too, Brendan. I love you more than my own life. You know that, don't you?"

The little boy grinned broadly. "Yep, I do."

Four

THE LIGHT OUTSIDE HER WINDOW shifted from bright, golden afternoon to cool blue within the span of a minute, and Celeste glanced up from her iMac, yanked out of her work by the change. She hadn't marked the passage of time, too captivated by the photo manipulation of a young woman into a fantastical warrior queen for the book cover she'd been commissioned for only yesterday. How long had it been since she'd been so lost in her work?

"Too long," she murmured, leaning back in her chair and reaching her knitted hands above her head to stretch muscles stiffened by long hours of inactivity. After she dropped her hands, she rolled her shoulders and then her head and focused her gaze out the window above her desk.

It was just after four, but already the sun had sunk behind the western hills, casting the A-frame and its yard into shadow. She craned her head to see to the left. The eastern valley was still awash in the golden brilliance of afternoon, as were the peaks above, but the shadow of night stretched markedly toward them even in the few minutes she watched. The play of sharp light and shadow on the mountains south of the mouth of the Northstar Valley captivated her as the song currently emanating from her computer's speakers—Gregorian chants accompanied by a flute and set to a transfixing beat—infused the moment with a spiritual tranquility.

Her gaze shifted to her snowboard and skis leaning in the corner of her office alcove. True to his word, Brodie had brought them by first thing yesterday morning with a perfect new coat of wax that was sure to send her shooting down the slopes with exhilarating speed.

Her lips curved. *Brodie.*

"Crap!"

She leapt to her feet, sending her chair rolling across the floor. Bard, who was curled in his usual place in front of the fire, darted for the safety beneath the chair she'd set by the front door and regarded her with lamp-like blue eyes narrowed in annoyance.

"Sorry," she muttered. She returned the computer chair to her desk and snatched her boots from beside the fire where she'd left them to dry after her walk before lunch. Then she bent down to pet her cat, who seemed to have forgiven her outburst already; he hopped up on the chair to make it easier for her to pet him. "I gotta go, Bard, but I shouldn't be gone too long."

She darted through the house, grabbing her parka from its hook in the mudroom on her way out the door.

The truck Ty and Shannon had lent her started like a champ, and she made a mental note to thank them again the next time she saw them, because at twelve degrees, her car would've given her trouble. By the time she reached the bottom of Lightning Ridge Road, she was even more grateful for the truck's four-wheel drive. The road was steep where it descended the north side of the ridge through the conifer forest. Brodie had plowed and sanded the road, but as he'd warned, it was still slick. When she turned left onto the road up to the ski hill, she lifted her hands in turns and flexed her fingers to work out the ache from gripping her steering wheel so tightly.

"You'd think I'd never driven in snow before," she muttered.

She'd driven the truck up to the A-frame, but this was her first trip down—Shannon had driven her the few times she'd left the cabin since moving into it Saturday morning—so she was probably being unfair to herself. Maybe tomorrow she should follow Ty's suggestion and drive the truck around in the snow on the Bar E Ranch to get used to how it handled. At least there she'd have help if she got into trouble. That thought forced her to admit that it was nice to know she had support here even if she was out of the habit of asking for or accepting it. As much as she wanted and needed to handle this mess on her own, it felt good to know she didn't *have* to like she had during the first two months after Marc's death.

The road up to the ski lodge wasn't much better than the one down from her cabin, but it was wider, and she didn't feel *quite* so panicky. Even so, when she parked near the tall metal-grate stairs up to the lodge, she rested her head on the steering wheel for a moment. Other fears replaced the tension of her drive, and she had to fight the urge to back out of the spot and head right back to the cabin. She didn't need a job at the ski hill. Money was tight, but it wasn't *that* tight, and she'd be able to buy a season pass next week or the week after. The idea of having to deal with people even a few days a week and the possibility of exploding at them like she had at her assistant at Liberty Bay Advertising paralyzed her. She couldn't face that again. And yet… the thought of sequestering herself in the cabin—cozy and lovely as it was—wasn't any more appealing. In fact, her heart jumped and raced erratically again. She hadn't come to Northstar to go on hiding.

"I'm tired of being afraid."

That admission spurred her anger, and she bolted upright, scowling. Marc was dead. There was nothing she could do about that, and she had to stop letting it terrorize her.

Taking a deep breath, she stepped out of the truck with her spine stubbornly straight and climbed the metal grate stairs to the lodge. At the top, she stopped in her tracks. She had no idea where she was supposed to go, where she might find Brodie, or what his father looked like. Glancing toward the ski shop, the last place she'd seen Brodie at work on the hill, she saw a "closed" sign in the window of the door. Someone in the lodge would surely know where he was, so she entered through the door straight ahead from the top of the stairs. The bottom floor was a locker room with a counter that connected to the ski shop, currently shuttered. She headed upstairs to the lodge's small restaurant and immediately recognized the redhead behind the counter preoccupied with a clipboard. Inventory, no doubt, to get ready for the opening of the ski hill.

Ainsley Dunn was, as Celeste had first thought, a strikingly beautiful woman with delicate features, a dusting of freckles across her ivory skin, and long hair that looked like highly polished copper. When she realized she wasn't alone, Ainsley glanced up, meeting Celeste's gaze with her crystalline blue eyes and a broad smile.

"Celeste, right?"

She nodded. "Hi again, Ainsley."

"You wouldn't be looking for my brother, would you?"

"I am, yes."

"He's out on the bunny hill running the snow machine. He should be about done for the day, if you want to wait, or you can just head out there."

"I'll, uh… I'll just wait out front."

"You sure? It's pretty cold out today."

"Yeah. I need to acclimate."

Ainsley shrugged. "If you change your mind, the door'll be open 'til we all leave."

"Thanks."

Celeste found a bench made from snowboards just outside the lodge with a commanding view of the eastern Northstar Mountains framed by the tall, narrow evergreens at the edges of the ski hill's parking lot. The valley was now completely in the shadow of the western ridges, but those eastern hills and peaks were awash in vivid rose where the sun touched them and deep lavender where it didn't. A breeze swirled in from the north, chilling the bare skin of her face, and its sharpness was invigorating. If there was one benefit to having no desire to engage in her artistic pursuits, it was that she wasn't plagued by the restless need to translate every detail of what she saw, smelled, heard, and felt onto paper. Instead, she was free to enjoy the moment with all her senses. Free to simply *be*.

Her eyes slid closed, and she focused on the scent of pine and sage muted by the cold and on the touch of wintry air on her face. A fine flurry of snow from the snow machine wafted over the lodge to curl around her, tickling her cheeks like feathers of ice. The snow machine's engine stopped, plunging her into silence, and as the sound faded from her ears' memory, quieter, natural sounds infiltrated her—the twittering of chickadees in the trees over by the lift to her left, the hoarse screech of a Stellar's jay, and the gentle sighing of the frigid wind through the boughs of the pines and firs. When she listened more closely, she even heard the hissing of snow over snow as it drifted with the wind along the ground.

She'd been right to come here. She needed this peace to reconnect with herself and the elements, to clear her mind of the trauma of Marc's death and the events that precipitated it.

I'll be okay, she thought, and for the first time in months, she believed she would be. Not today or this week or even this month, but eventually.

"Stay out here much longer in this wind and we won't have to commission an ice sculpture for Christmas this year because we'll have a Celeste-cicle."

She jumped at the sound of his voice… but barely, and when she swiveled on the bench toward him, her lips were lifted in a smile.

Clad in ski pants and jacket with his feet stuffed into snowboard boots and a knit hat covering his auburn hair, Brodie was the image of a snowboarder even without a board strapped to his feet. So was the bright-eyed boy standing next to him. Brendan, she guessed. Other than having brown hair instead of red, he was exactly how she imagined Brodie would've looked at that age. Her heart did a funny thing, seeing them together—fluttered with a maternal appreciation she'd done her best to bury deep.

"You're a riot, Brodie," she retorted.

"I try." He grinned. "You could've waited inside if you didn't want to come get me."

"I know, but I wanted to enjoy the view."

"The view from the lodge is even better. And warmer."

"Maybe I wanted to enjoy the cold, too."

"And the solitude, I'm guessing." He glanced over his shoulder at the lodge, then back at Celeste. "I was beginning to wonder if you'd changed your mind about the job."

"Sorry about that. I got to working on a book cover, and I lost track of time."

"Nothing to be sorry about. That's your primary source of income." Brodie's expression was as good-humored as ever but softer somehow and became more so when he glanced down at his son. "Brendan, this is our new neighbor, Celeste."

The boy extended his mittened hand, and Celeste shook it. "Pleasure to meet you," he said.

"The pleasure's all mine, Brendan. You board?"

"Papa's teaching me. That's why we've been making

snow—so I can practice on the bunny hill for a few days before the hill opens."

"Must be pretty awesome to have your very own ski hill."

"Oh, yeah! I got to ski lots last year, and this year I'll get to go down a couple of the big runs on my snowboard instead of being stuck on the bunny hill."

"Good for you! I'll bet you can't wait."

Brendan grinned, looking ever more like his father. The flutter turned into a squeeze. Would her own child have been as excited for the start of ski season? As soon as the question formed, she smashed it. *That* was a door she couldn't afford to open right now or any time soon. *Focus on one tragedy at a time*, she reminded herself.

"So, how long you gonna be renting Fred's cabin?" Brendan inquired.

"A couple months at least. Maybe longer. I don't know yet."

"You'll be here for Christmas?"

"That's the plan. I'm going to spend Christmas with my friends, Ty and Shannon."

"But won't your family miss you?"

"Shannon and Ty *are* family to me. Besides, I don't have much family *to* miss me—just my mom and Grandma Letty, and I wouldn't have seen them this year, anyhow."

"How come?"

"Grandma Letty is going on a well-deserved cruise to the Caribbean with her best friend."

"What about your mom?"

Celeste's smile faded. "She moved back to California this spring, and she doesn't have a place for me to stay or the money to come visit me."

"Couldn't you—"

"Brendan," Brodie interrupted. "That's enough questions for now. Why don't you run inside and tell Granddad that Celeste is here. We'll be up in a minute."

"Okay!" the boy piped and zipped into the lodge.

Celeste let out a breath in relief. Brendan was an adorable kid, and there had been a day not so long ago when she would've gladly spent hours listening to him talk and answering his questions, but even the innocent topics of family and Christmas were too tender for her to talk about. Brodie met her gaze with a sympathetic smile, and it was obvious he'd sensed her distress.

"He calls you Papa," she murmured. "That's adorable."

His lips twitched upward. "And his favorite game is twenty questions. Can you tell?"

She nodded. "He's a beautiful boy, Brodie."

"He gets that from his mother."

"I'm pretty sure he gets it from you. I wish...." She closed her mouth, pressed her lips together and tried again. "I hope I'll get to a place before I head back to Washington that I can sit down and play twenty questions with him."

"He'd like that. In the meantime, let's head in, introduce you to my dad, and figure out if you for sure want the job and *what* job you want so we can close up shop before midnight."

"Sorry," she mumbled again. "I don't mean to drag your work day out."

"You aren't, and even if you were, you wouldn't hear me complain about it. The ski hill isn't work to me. It's play, and who's ever in a hurry to stop playing?"

"Well met."

"Come on in."

Brodie held the door for her and followed her up the stairs to the restaurant, then led her to the office to the left of the kitchen. A bear of a man in his mid fifties with keen but welcoming green eyes leaned against the desk in the center of the room poring over a clipboard—perhaps the inventory list Ainsley had been working on when Celeste had first arrived. His rich red hair was only beginning to show a little silver, and with that heavily muscled, thick-boned frame, it would be many years yet before he began the decline from his prime. She'd thought Brodie had a brawny build, but next to his father, he was considerably lighter.

"Dad, this is Celeste. Celeste, meet my father, Angus Dunn."

"Welcome," Angus said, extending a huge hand in greeting.

Celeste gripped his hand and shook it. "Thank you."

"Come on, Brendan," Brodie said to his son. "Let's go help Aunt Ainsley finish up."

As Brendan followed his father out of the office, Celeste heard him say, "You're right, Papa. She *is* kinda sad. But I like her."

Over her shoulder, she watched them disappear around the corner and frowned. Sad was the simple way to put it—simple enough for a five-year-old to grasp—but it was an umbrella term for what she really was. Bitter. Despondent. Hollow.

"Brodie says he offered ye a job."

Celeste returned her attention to Brodie's father. Despite all his years away from Scotland, Angus hadn't lost his charming accent, and she couldn't help but smile. "Yes, sir."

"None a'that 'sir' business, lass. Angus'll be jus' fine. The job's yers if ye wan' it. Twelve bucks an hour with a free season pass. I understand ye're not interested in full time because you're already self-employed and doing well enough to support yerself with it. Good on ye. I admire that spirit."

"Thank you," Celeste murmured. "You don't want references or a list of my qualifications before you offer me the job?"

"Brodie's the real power here—I'm just the boss on paper—an' he wants ye here, which is enough recommendation for me, but yer friend Shannon was plenty helpful as well. Said ye were the captain of yer ski team in high school an' ye won a few awards at university." With his hands braced on the desk behind him, he studied her with narrowed eyes, and she squirmed, feeling like he was looking into the deepest, most protected part of her soul. "Ye don't need the job for the money, but I suspect ye need it for something else. So. What are ye interested in doin' round here?"

Of course Shannon had stuck her nose in it. Celeste smiled and reminded herself to add that to her list of things she needed to thank her friend for later. Angus was right. While the extra money would be nice, she didn't *need* it, but she *did* need the reason to leave her house and she needed the social interaction. And since all that came with a free season lift ticket, what more could she ask for? Suddenly, her earlier doubts fell silent, revealed for the unhealthy and baseless fears they were. "Whatever you need help with. I'm flexible."

Angus laughed, a rich, deep sound that brought another, firmer smile to her face. "I think ye an' I are gonna get along tremendously, lass. Brodie'll let ye know when we're going to open the hill, an' ye can work with him to figure out a schedule ye're comfortable with."

"Thank you, Angus. I mean that."

"I believe ye."

When she left the office with paperwork to fill out for taxes and whatnot, she found Brendan sitting at a table near the windows, which had an incredible view as Brodie had said. The boy's father was stocking the rack of chips near the cash register.

"I feel I owe you dinner at least," she said, ambling over, "so if you're in the mood, why don't you come over for dinner and cash in that rain check."

"I would love to, but Mum and Dad have plans tonight, so they won't be able to watch Brendan for me."

"Bring him with you."

"I do that and I won't be able to get a word in edgewise. Saturday when he's at his mom's would be better. Then we'd be free to be however spontaneous we wanted."

"Saturday would be great. Do you have any special requests? Or anything you won't eat?"

"I'm not picky."

"You sure about that?"

"Yep."

"So, if I make gyoza, you'll eat them?"

"What're gyoza?"

"Japanese potstickers."

"If they're anything like Chinese potstickers, I'll love them."

"They're similar, but I like them better. Or I could make something Italian."

"That'd be great, too."

"Something tells me you'd answer the same way even if I said I was going to cook squid."

"My nana taught me never to question the cook."

"Wise woman."

"Yes, she is. What time on Saturday? And do I need to dress up?"

"Six? And no, I'd rather you came as your usual charming and casual self."

"Perfect. See ya then if not before."

The way he said it made her feel like he was hoping he'd see her before. She offered him a smile in return and bid him and Brendan good night, then headed downstairs and out of the lodge. As she navigated down the ski hill driveway and up the icy Lightning Ridge Road, she thought back on his answer to her invitation to bring Brendan along. At face value, the way he'd couched it in an insinuation that his son would put a damper on anything romantic sounded like a man who wanted to focus solely on his prospective lover, but she sensed there was more to it. In his place, she would want to wait a while before she included her child in a new relationship; it would be doubly heartbreaking if the child got attached only to have the relationship end, and she'd want to know she could trust her boyfriend with her child, to be certain that he wasn't cruel or violent.

Or unstable. Like me right now.

In Brodie's place, she'd be hesitant to let Brendan spend much time with her, too.

* * *

When his knock received no answer, Brodie turned the knob on the outer back door of Celeste's cabin and was a little surprised to find it unlocked; she struck him as the cautious type. He stepped inside and set the canvas grocery sack he'd brought with him on the coat rack bench so he could have both hands free to take off his coat and boots. Music drifted to his ears from within the cabin, and he thought he recognized Enigma's Amis-infused *Return to Innocence.* He smiled, both enjoying the song and the memory of their brief conversation about their respective tastes in music. The mood-music, as his mother called it, suited her.

With his boots off and tucked into one of the cubbyholes beneath the bench and his coat hanging on the hook above them, he picked up his sack and knocked on the inner door of the cabin. Seconds later, she opened it, and immediately her face brightened. That was a promising sign. He glanced over the rest of her. Instead of the black he'd expected, she was wearing snug-fitting blue jeans and a tunic-length cable knit sweater with a deep V-neck that was the color of pink champagne. She'd painted her nails to match, and she wore a little makeup as well, with a touch of burgundy in that smoky-eye thing she'd created with an artist's finesse. A slender crescent moon studded with clear stones—diamonds or something cheaper, he had no idea— hung around her neck on a delicate gold chain, understated but elegant. She was dressed as casually as he was, but he felt shabby standing next to her.

The warm tones of her ensemble drew attention to the softness of her skin and brought out the richness of her eyes, and he stood on the threshold of her temporary home in danger of being swallowed by them. It was going to be one hell of a ride discovering the secrets behind them. *Jings, crivens, and help ma boab.*

"What?" she asked, noticing his perusal.

"You're wearing… color."

She lowered her gaze with a shyness he hadn't yet seen and stepped aside so he could come in. "Yeah. I didn't feel like wearing black tonight."

"Color me stupefied. You look stunning. You always do, but this…. The artist in you is coming out."

More color flushed her cheeks, and he decided to let the matter go before he pushed her too far. He was determined to peel back a few more of her layers tonight while he had her all to himself, and he wouldn't get anywhere with her if he triggered her devil-may-care apathy. He stepped around her into the kitchen, set his sack on the island between it and the living room, and pulled out the bottle of white zinfandel. "I know you said I didn't need to bring anything when I asked yesterday, but Mum thought I should bring *something.*"

"I don't drink."

The sudden cold tremble in her voice jerked his attention to her. She stared at the bottle with an odd light in her eyes. Not quite terror or revulsion, but close enough that he was reminded of a frightened doe again. He filed the information away for later. When she lifted her gaze to meet his, she forced her lips into a smile, but it took a moment for her eyes to catch up.

"It was very thoughtful of you and your mother," she said, "and I appreciate the gesture. You're more than welcome to drink it."

"I don't drink much myself. A beer once in a rare while's about it." He tucked the bottle back into his sack and pulled out the hot cider fixings he'd brought as a back up, noting how she visibly relaxed. "This is much more my style."

"Now, *that* is an excellent choice of beverage. Have a seat on the couch while I finish the gyoza."

"Mind if I sit here at the island instead?"

"Help yourself, but if you're in the way, you might get put to work."

"Fine by me." He perched on one of the stools to watch her work. "Now that you've been in Northstar a full week, how are you liking it?"

"I'm loving it. Although, sadly, with as much work as I've had, I haven't had as much chance to get out and explore as I'd like. I'm hoping that will change in the next week or so once I get caught up. Know of any particularly good trails for cross-country skiing?"

"I know a ton."

While she worked, they talked about the best trails. She had already prepared the filling for the potstickers using ground chicken, she explained, rather than the pork many people preferred because she didn't eat pork—why didn't that surprise him?—and now set out the wonton wrappers on a big cutting board. He watched as she first spooned the filling onto the wrappers and then folded them over into triangles and pressed the edges together, occasionally dipping her fingers into the bowl of water beside the cutting board. She had such graceful hands, and the speed with which she worked made him believe she'd made these more than a few times.

"You're almost as fast at making gyoza as Lindsay Hammond is."

"Lindsay Hammond?" Celeste asked, glancing at him briefly as she set the first batch aside and started the next.

"She's another Kitsap County transplant. We have a few here in Northstar."

"That's right. She used to be Lindsay Miller, right?"

"Right. She's catering for the Ramshorn's events these days and well on her way to opening her own business."

"You said she makes gyoza?"

"Almost exactly like you do, except that she uses pork. It's one of her most asked-for dishes, and with good reason. They're amazing."

Celeste paused in her task to regard him with her lips twisted in amusement. "So you knew *exactly* what I was talking about on Tuesday when I invited you over, even before I clarified."

He grinned. "Guilty as charged. I have a bad habit of making light of just about everything."

"So I've noticed. But that's not such a bad thing."

"You say that now, lass, but just wait. It'll get on your nerves. Always does."

"We'll see. I could use that kind of lightheartedness right now," she said quietly, averting her gaze and returning to her task.

I bet you can.

Brodie watched as she first fried and then briefly

steamed the gyoza and started the hot cider with a fluid confidence. Her ease in the kitchen led him to believe that she tended to turn any task into art, practicing it until she could make something mundane into something beautiful. Before he knew it, dinner was ready, and she was pulling plates and flatware out. He took the dishes from her and set them out.

"Mind if I ask why you offered to cook us dinner rather than letting me take you out for our first date?" he inquired lightly as they sat down to eat.

"I owe you, remember? I can't pay back a debt by letting you take me out."

"That's a matter of semantics. I see it like you agreeing to go out with me is doing me a favor rather than the other way around."

"Oh, you're not so bad, Brodie," she teased. "Surely you can't be *that* desperate."

He ignored decorum and braced his elbows on the table with his chin resting on his folded hands. "Oh yeah? I am thirty-one years old and the longest relationship I've had lasted less than a year and a half. Most ended after a couple months."

"Over a year is respectable."

"Sure it is… except that it probably wouldn't have lasted more than four months if she hadn't gotten pregnant."

"That was Brendan's mom?" With a delightfully wicked gleam in her eyes, she asked, "Or do you have more kids out there?"

He chuckled. "That was Brendan's mom, and unless any of the others are hiding something from me, he's the only kid I have. Yet."

"You want more children?"

"Always have. I was never keen on a big brood, but two or three would be nice. I've loved having siblings, and I think Brendan would make a great big brother."

"I'll bet he would."

"What about you?"

The humor faded from her eyes, and he sensed children were a tender topic. Why? When she answered his question, he was surprised.

"I always thought I'd have two or three."

He was curious to know if she still thought that or if whatever had happened to her had chased that idea away, but he was also smart enough to know that he was already treading on thin ice with the subject, so he didn't press her.

"I'm sorry I asked you to bring Brendan," she said, redirecting the conversation as he'd figured she'd want to. "I understand why you said no."

"It's nothing personal, Celeste, and believe it or not, I like the fact that it was so natural to you to want to include him. Says a lot about you." Deciding their conversation was darkening too much, he laughed. "Isn't it usually the other way around? Isn't it usually the single mom in search of a nurturing man?"

"Only because there are more single moms," she replied a little less solemnly. "I imagine any parent, regardless of gender, would want to know their children are safe with any prospective mate."

"True enough."

"I'd love to hear more about him, if that's all right with you. What else does he like other than snowboarding and skiing?"

"We could talk about anything under the stars, and you want to talk about my son?"

"He's a big part of who you are, and I like the way your expression gentles when you talk about him. It shows a different side of you I haven't seen much of yet."

That was definitely *not* the response he'd expected. He'd thought she'd use Brendan as a way to keep the conversation off her, and her interest in what was most important to him further incited his curiosity about her. For now, he went with her choice of topic, and his narrative, fueled and guided by her questions, carried them through the rest of their mouthwatering meal and the dishes after. They worked seamlessly together in tidying up the kitchen, and he liked that. Even at the height of his relationship with Stephanie, they'd never had that level of harmony.

When they retreated to the couch—him on the middle cushion with one arm draped over the back and his right ankle resting on his left knee and her curled up against the arm with her feet tucked under her—the conversation shifted to their education. He knew she'd attended the University of Washington with Shannon and that that was how the two friends had met, but it was fun listening to her talk about their adventures at school together. That was the one aspect of college Brodie regretted missing out on—the social interactions and the opportunity to test the waters of adulthood in the relative familiarity of a school environment. Still, he hadn't done so bad for himself. He had two stable jobs and an income that met all his needs and most of his wants, a son he adored even if Brendan's arrival in his life hadn't come about the way he'd planned, with a marriage to a woman he wanted to grow old with, and Northstar provided a wealth of good friends.

At some point, he glanced toward the front door, his attention drawn to it by what sounded like meowing. He couldn't be sure as music still played from Celeste's computer, but he asked about it.

"Oh, Bard must want in," she replied, bouncing to her feet.

"Bard?"

"My cat."

"He wouldn't be a big lad with long black hair and the most incredible blue eyes I've ever seen on a cat, would he?"

Celeste didn't need to answer. As soon as she opened the door, the cat he'd spotted more than once roaming through the A-frame's yard strolled inside.

"Yes, he would," Brodie remarked.

The cat put his paws on Celeste's knees, and she picked him up and carried him to the couch, reclaiming her spot. Bard's purr could be heard even over the music. After a moment, the feline left Celeste's lap and padded across the short distance between her and Brodie to sniff his master's guest. Then, with an unmistakable demand to be petted, Bard head-butted Brodie's jaw.

"Friendly lad, aren't you," Brodie whispered and indulged the cat. Moon and Binx would surely make him pay for this later, but he could no more resist Bard's command than he could theirs. They'd just have to deal with it. "So, Bard like Shakespeare's nickname or Bard like Bard the Bowman from *The Hobbit*?"

"Both, but more Bard the Bowman."

Brodie glanced at her and found her observing him with a frown. "Why are you looking at me like that?"

"He likes you."

"I'm pretty sure I have 'sucker' scribbled across my forehead in ink every animal can see." Brodie scratched under the cat's chin and narrowed his eyes as he studied Celeste's expression. "You say that like it's odd he would like me."

"He doesn't like men. So far you and Ty are the only two I've seen him not only approach but… well, make a fool of himself over."

"It's that 'sucker' tattoo. Ty's got it, too. Why do you think he's such a gifted horse trainer? Animals are smart."

"Yes, they are," she murmured. Abruptly, she smiled. "I'm going to go out on a limb and say you have pets. How many?"

"Two dogs and two cats, all rescues. The dogs are Labs, a black female and a yellow male, named Charlie and Jake, and the cats are Moon and Binx. Moon, as you might guess, is white, and Binx is black like the cat in *Hocus Pocus*, which is where he got his name."

"I love that."

Eventually, Bard decided food was of greater importance than affection and leapt off the couch in search of his bowl. Brodie turned their conversation onto a topic he was curious about and figured would be safe.

"Tell me more about what you do for a living."

"I design covers for self-published authors and craft things for my Etsy store—everything from pottery to jewelry to bridal headpieces."

"Do you have any you could show me?"

"Nothing for the Etsy store—I just sent out my last order yesterday—but I have pictures, and I could show you some of the book covers I've done. They're displayed on my website."

"I'd love to see them."

She bounced to her feet, and he followed her over to her computer, waiting patiently behind her chair while the machine started up. It took a surprising amount of willpower not to settle his hand on her shoulder while she navigated to her website or to comb her hair back from her face. Then her home on the web loaded, and she gave him a tour first through her covers and then through her crafts. He didn't know if pagan was the correct term, but it was the one that came to mind as he took in the digital representation of her portfolio. Whatever it was, a connection to nature was distinctly evident in her work, and it was beautiful. Each and every piece was exquisite, whether it was a vibrant, magic-themed cover for a fantasy novel he would never have known wasn't the product of a major publisher if she hadn't told him or a sprite-inspired bridal crown with raw crystal points connected by graceful sterling silver vines. He particularly liked a silver ring she'd made and set with a garnet Ty and Shannon had found east of Devyn last summer, and he liked the gentle pleasure that infiltrated her voice when she admitted that she hadn't wanted to sell that one.

"You are an incredibly gifted artist, lass," he murmured.

He didn't realize he was leaning low over her shoulder to get a better view of her computer screen until she turned in her chair to face him. She was so close, and he saw the shy intent in her eyes half a second before she acted on it.

Her lips were soft but searching and tasted faintly of spiced cider, and it was only a moment before his shock gave way to sudden and intense desire. He took her hand and helped her to her feet, needing more, and when she rocked her body into his, he groaned. Maybe the length of time since he'd last kissed a woman had made him forget how it could make his body hum in anticipation of more, but he suspected it was Celeste. She was coy and confident at the same time, first giving him the control and then snatching it away.

When they broke apart, they were both breathless. She searched his face with surprise and wonder in her eyes, and Brodie gave in to temptation and tucked her hair behind her ears. His heart pounded harder when her eyes fluttered closed and she leaned into his touch. He folded his arms around her, sensing when she rested her head on his chest that she needed a moment to digest what had just transpired or perhaps to regain her balance.

Her computer's screensaver came on, snagging his attention, and after a moment of irritation at the distraction, he paid closer attention to the photos displayed. They weren't, as he would have thought, nature shots. Instead, they showcased Celeste and her friends and family. He recognized Shannon in many of them, and two women he guessed were her mother and grandmother. There were other women, probably her friends from Washington, and a couple with Ty and Shannon's brother, Pat. In every photo, he noted, Celeste had long hair, so he assumed the chin-length cut was a recent style change. Something tickled his brain, but it was too elusive for him to decipher.

"Why aren't there any men in your photos other than Pat and Ty?" The question was out of his mouth before he had a chance to question the wisdom of asking it.

"The women in my family don't have much luck with men," she murmured.

A shot of her smiling at the camera over her shoulder with her long, dark hair spilling down her back from under a knit hat slid onto the computer's screen. He recognized the Northstar Ski Hill lodge behind her, and he jerked back as a memory snapped into focus. She reacted similarly, but confusion shadowed her face.

"You were here last Christmas," he said, "to visit Shannon and Ty, and you had a man with you. You were married."

She glanced at the computer screen just in time to catch a glimpse of the photo before another one replaced it. Then she walked over to the couch and sat primly on the edge of the cushion with her hands folded in her lap.

"I'm not still married, if that's what spooked you," she said quietly.

Brodie eyed her for a moment, noted the way she met his gaze briefly before lowering her eyes to her hands. Shame and a darker emotion he had no hope of naming erased the wonder that had widened her eyes just a few minutes ago, and he missed it dearly. Hoping he might find a way to bring it back, he sat on the couch beside her, facing her.

"What happened?"

"It ended."

Defiance firmed her voice and burned in her eyes,

and he watched that to-hell-with-it rashness click into place.

"From the sounds of it, you're glad it did."

"It was a relief."

But in some ways not, he guessed. "Now that I've thoroughly spoiled the evening, maybe I should call it a night."

"No," she replied quickly with a trace of regret in her voice. "Please don't. Don't leave on that kind of note. I feel like the fact that I was married just completely turned you off."

"Far from it," he assured her. "But I feel bad for dredging up what is obviously still a tender subject."

"Everything's a tender subject with me anymore."

"Is that why you have pictures of people on your screensaver instead of nature shots?"

"How did you...?"

"All your artwork has ties to the natural world, and you yourself exude this...." He paused, searching for the word, then smiled as he recalled what she had said about his sister a week ago. "You have this *fawn-like* quality about you, which tells me you're introverted and prefer nature to people. So, I'm going to head home and let you unwind and recharge."

The war between relief and disappointment that played out across her face might've been comical if he hadn't only just caught her in a vulnerable moment. He took her hand and squeezed, then stood.

"Thank you for dinner, for sharing your artwork with me, and for the kiss. We'll have to try it again sometime."

"Which part?"

"All of it."

She walked with him to the door. As he stepped into the mudroom, he noticed a small notecard tacked to the doorframe with a scattering of tiny, colorful butterflies. The words, penned in elegant script, said, *I will not be the damsel in distress. I will save myself.*

After seeing her artwork, he didn't doubt Celeste was the artist behind it. Besides, motivational quips weren't old Fred's style.

Whatever battle she's been thrown into, at least she's fighting it. Or trying to.

Brodie quickly averted his gaze and took a seat on the bench, hoping she hadn't noticed his pause; that little placard was deeply personal, and he didn't want her to feel like he was invading her privacy. She leaned against the doorjamb and waited while he pulled his boots and coat on, and before he left, he kissed her again. Some of the magic of their first kiss had faded, as he'd known it would, but it was still potent enough to kick start his pulse.

He walked home beneath a star-spattered sky, more sure than ever that he neither wanted to nor could stay away from Celeste. She was as fragile right now as a delicate blade of hoarfrost, and rebuilding her strength would require a finesse he wasn't sure he possessed, but he had to try. If it could be done, she was likely to be the woman he'd always pictured himself settling down with. Even if she wasn't, he'd made a promise to never let a wounded heart suffer alone.

Glancing at the stars before he stepped into his house, he muttered, "Yeah, I hear you, Inez."

Five

CELESTE INSPECTED THE COVER one last time to check for errors in the text that she might have missed and to make sure it was exactly as she'd envisioned when she'd read the author's descriptions of what he wanted, then opened her mail app, attached the proof file, and sent it off for his approval. Her calendar app hopped at the bottom of her screen, notifying her of an impending appointment. Frowning, she opened the app. The first event was the Evergreen Writers Conference, which would begin tomorrow and run all day, but it was the second that elicited a shriek.

Seattle Fashion Show. All day.

Marc had received a late invitation to attend the show when another designer had backed out, and he'd asked her to model the dresses he'd be featuring. She shoved her chair back from her desk in a panic as his words echoed in her mind, and it tipped over, sending her sprawling to the floor.

"What the fuck do you mean you can't do it?"

She'd been planning to attend the writers conference for almost a year with the hope that she'd be able to pick up some clients from the indie authors who would be in attendance—authors who were rocketing into the stratosphere of the publishing world after the introduction of Amazon's self-publishing platform. If she could snag a few, it would give her fledgling cover-design business an explosive start. He'd *known* about it for months; she hadn't been able to stop talking about it. But she understood now that knowing about it and caring about it were two different things to him.

With her breaths coming in too shallow and fast, she crawled over to the couch and sat on the floor with her back against it and her knees pulled up to her chest, wincing at the memory of each shattering crash. He picked up one piece after another and hurled them in every direction in his mindless wrath. Vases, bowls, jewelry pieces that each represented hours of work flew across her bright, airy studio in his rage, smashing against walls, windows, and worktables. Not one piece escaped, and he broke half the windows as well.

Tears rolled silently down her face, and she hugged her knees tightly to ward off the terror. Alerted to her distress, Bard crawled onto her knees and pushed his way into her arms. She hugged him close, anchored in the present by his loud purring and his silky fur. He'd been the shining light on that dark day, too—the day when Marcus Lamb, talented clothing designer with an irresistible charisma, had brutally revealed the dark side he'd hidden from her and from the world. She shuddered, recalling the way his face had turned crimson with veins protruding and contorting that handsome visage into something hideous.

Her studio had been destroyed, and it had taken her a full week to clean up the mess and sort through what was left of her supplies for anything salvageable. Worse than the destruction, she'd had to notify clients and customers of her inability to fill their orders. She'd lied and said a tree had fallen on her studio and destroyed everything and that it would be weeks before she'd be able to make everything again. Thankfully, most of her customers and clients had been understanding, but a few had opted for a refund rather than waiting for her to complete a new piece for them.

She'd stood her ground and refused to cancel her plans, but it had cost her dearly, and she couldn't call it a victory, because in the end, neither of them won. He'd died a couple months later and she'd backed out of the conference shortly after when it became clear there was no way she'd be able to pull herself together enough to schmooze potential clients. He could've picked any one of the two dozen young women who would've jumped at the chance to model for him, but instead, he'd let his need to control everything in his life ignite his temper, and they'd both missed out on opportunities that could have taken their careers to whole new levels. She might yet find other opportunities, but Marc never would.

The familiar numbness crept over her, and as the fear and anger receded, she embraced it even though she knew it was dangerous to do so. She didn't like the detached emptiness of it, but at least she could function better than she could in the thrall of terror.

She gave Bard a few more scratches under the chin and set him on the couch. Methodically, she righted her chair, pulled it back to her desk and sat in it to clear every last reminder of Marc from her computer. There weren't too many as she'd already gone through it a couple times, but it still took her almost an hour to sort through all the files and apps.

With that chore done, she tipped her head back against her chair as more of those silent, numb tears slipped from her eyes. *How long is that bastard going to haunt me?*

When the phone rang, she habitually glanced at her cell phone, which hadn't been turned on since she'd arrived in Northstar—blissfully, there was no service here—and it was a moment before her wits fired and started and she realized it was the cabin's landline. She picked up the cordless, which she'd set on her desk when she'd settled in to work dark and early this morning.

"Hello?" she asked.

"It's Brodie."

The breath she hadn't realized she'd been holding rushed out of her lungs. "Brodie. Hi. How are you?"

He hesitated a moment before responding. "I'm fine, but are you all right?"

Damn, the man was insightful, which meant he'd see right through a lie. "I'm okay now. Just had a moment."

"Well, I have something that might cheer you up. The snow we've had the last couple days put us over the top, so we're opening the hill tomorrow."

"Do you need me to come in to work?"

"Tomorrow being Thursday, I don't expect we'll be

too busy. I'm calling to invite you to hit the slopes with me and the rest of my family while they're still one-hundred-percent pristine."

Still a little shaky from her episode, she almost said no. But, with the curious effect Brodie had on her, she heard herself say, "I'd love to. When?"

"As soon as you can get your gear together and get up here."

"See you in half an hour, then." She grinned, anticipation pulsing delightfully through her. "Or less."

After Brodie had dropped off her freshly waxed snowboard and skis last Tuesday, she'd gathered all her gear together and piled it on the work bench in the mudroom so she wouldn't have to waste time searching for everything when the call came that the ski hill was open. All she had to do was change into something easier to stuff into her snow pants get her rear safely down Lightning Ridge Road and up to the ski hill. She dug a pair of soft leggings out of her dresser in the loft and a ribbed sweater that fit close to her curves and would disallow any breezes to steal away her body heat.

She gave Bard some attention and checked his food and water bowls, stoked the fire and closed the damper, and stepped out the door into the mudroom, catching sight of the notecard she'd tacked to the doorframe right at her eye level.

I will not be the damsel in distress. I will save myself.

She'd made it her first day in the cabin after everyone had left using the supplies Ty and Shannon had given her, and though she hadn't been able to get any more elaborate than the tiny butterflies, it was *something*, a firm step toward reclaiming her life and her zeal for art.

I will uphold that, she promised herself as she sat on the bench to pull her snow boots on. *And taking a few runs down the mountain with Brodie is a fine start.*

She hadn't been skiing since that day at the Northstar Ski Hill with Marc, Ty, and Shannon last Christmas, and before that, she and Marc had been too busy pushing their careers to take much time to hit the slopes. Her lack of skiing and snowboarding the last couple years made the promise of enjoying the untouched powder all the sweeter, and she grabbed her bags and zipped out the door. The excitement that hummed through her was marvelously refreshing, and she drove with more confidence than she'd had even a week ago down the icy road.

Brodie was waiting for her in the locker room just inside the front door of the lodge with his entire family. They were already trussed up, but the men were *not* in snow pants and jackets. Brodie and his father wore traditional Scottish kilts of a matching deep sky-blue, yellow, navy, and white plaid, and the two women wore sashes of the same plaid over their snow pants. It had to be their family tartan.

"I hope you boys aren't going fully traditional under those kilts," she remarked quietly to Brodie.

"Of course we are."

"But won't that be a little… *cold?*"

"All the more incentive to stay upright."

Angus and Ainsley greeted her with warm hugs as did the stately woman whom Celeste was certain, without being told, was Brodie's mother. Mrs. Dunn had the same inquisitive blue eyes as Brodie and Ainsley and the same delicate features that made her daughter so strikingly beautiful. Her silvering golden hair was tied back in waist-length braid that made Celeste miss her long hair—not for the first time. She combed her hand back through her hair, suddenly self-conscious about its lack of length.

"You've met the rest of my family," Brodie said, "but this beautiful lady here is the poor woman who brought me into this world, my mother, Sula Dunn. Short for Ursula. Like the sea witch in *The Little Mermaid.*"

"Or Ursula K. Le Guin, author of one of my favorite books, *The Left Hand of Darkness,*" Celeste quipped. Noting that Sula wasn't in the least bothered by her son comparing her to the tentacled villain, she playfully added, "If you're looking to impress me, you might want to expand your references beyond Disney movies."

"Excuse me, but that is the first Disney movie I've referenced. And anyhow, I have an almost-six-year-old son. What do you expect?"

Celeste surprised herself when she laughed. Still smiling, she turned to the rest of his family. "If you're all here, who's running the lift and holding down the fort here at the lodge?"

"Two of our other employees," Sula replied. "We'll get out of here so you can get into your gear."

"You going to wait for us at the lift?" Brodie inquired.

Angus and Sula glanced between their son and Celeste and exchanged knowing grins.

"No, I don' think so, lad," Angus said, ushering his wife and daughter outside.

"That was about as subtle as a cannon," Celeste remarked.

"Yeah... subtlety is not one of my family's stronger traits."

Again, she laughed.

"That may be the quickest I've yet seen you shed the.... Well, it's not exactly shyness. More an unwillingness to interact with people. Looks like my invitation put you in a better mood than you were in when I called."

She stuck her tongue out at him, and he beamed in response.

"That right there, lass. We need more of that. Hurry up so we can get out there and tear up all that beautiful untouched snow."

She glanced at his feet, saw ski rather than snowboard boots, and set her snowboard bag aside in favor of her skis. "I figured you for more of a snowboarder," she remarked.

"Usually, but on days like today with the kind of powder we have, it's a ski day."

"That's usually how I decide, too."

In short order, she was ready to go. Brodie led the way over to the lift, and Celeste couldn't stop smiling as her body reveled in the familiar motions required to transport herself on skis. And what a stunning, clear-skied day! The snow was brilliantly white beneath the crystalline sun, and even through her tinted goggles, the sky was a deep, rich sapphire, and there wasn't a breath of wind to disturb the snow pillowed thick on the branches of the conifers.

"There's nothing that can compare to a day like this to make you feel alive," she said breathlessly seconds before she and Brodie were scooped up by the chair lift.

"I couldn't agree more, lass," he said, glancing over his shoulder. "Best view in Northstar, right there, though it's even better at the top."

She followed his gaze, and the breath sucked between her teeth. Last year, dense gray snow clouds and flurries had clung to the mountains the entire day, obscuring the view. Not so today.

The view out the cabin and lodge windows was incredible, but as the lift carried them higher up the mountain, the eastern Northstar Mountains seemed to rise with them, giving her a fuller appreciation of their height. All decked out in blue and dazzling white, they were nothing short of spectacular. Wonder filled her, demolishing every last shred of numbness left in the wake of her panic attack.

In this moment, short though it may be, she was free.

She faced forward again and let her eyes drift closed for a moment. The crisp air on her face, the cool of the shadow on her right cheek, the warm sun on her left, and the lightness of shedding the lead blanket of memories combined to give her the most incredible feeling of bliss. When she opened her eyes again, Brodie was still taking in the view. She glanced at the mountains again, then focused her attention on him. Pride and the same gentleness she'd previously thought was reserved for his son were thick in his expression, making him beautiful. He was generally an attractive man, more cute than outright handsome, but right now, he appealed more to her than even the most physically gorgeous man on the face of the planet. Shyly, she slipped her gloved hand around his and squeezed. He met her gaze, and though his lips barely moved, his eyes ignited with a tender smile that infiltrated her heart even deeper than the amazing view.

Resting her head on his shoulder, she murmured,

"Thank you."

"You are most welcome, lass."

When he laid his head on top of hers, she realized with a start what she'd done, and though she twitched out of habit, she didn't break the contact. Instead, she tilted her face toward his. He didn't need any further invitation, and half a moment later, when he pressed his lips to hers, she purred. She liked the way he kissed as if he were exploring her spirit as well as her mouth. It was so different from Marc's grasping, forceful kisses, which had more often than not left her breathless for the wrong reasons and had, until she'd kissed Brodie on their first date four days ago, begun to make her believe she didn't enjoy this gateway of intimacy. Instead of inspiring her to shy away in aversion as she often had with Marc, Brodie's kiss invited her to lean into him. She slid her hand over his bristly jaw—that was a wholly new sensation; Marc hadn't ever let his beard grow more than a couple days—to the back of his head as hunger for more burned through her. Letting desire take over, she dragged her hand down his neck and over his chest.

"Careful, lass," he murmured against her lips. "Don't go starting anything we can't finish right now."

Leaning away a little, she glanced over him, at his kilt and his bare knees below it, and a shimmer of feistiness wriggled through her. "Are you *really* naked under that thing?"

With a teasing grin, he slowly inched the material up his leg, revealing the hem of a pair of black boxers. They wouldn't offer much protection from the snow if he biffed it, but she figured that wasn't too likely. She swatted his arm.

"Liar."

"Not entirely. Dad actually *is* bare underneath, so you may not want to ski too close in case he eats powder. I'm pretty sure my mother is the only woman on earth who wants to see that show."

"You're going to let your dad out-man you?"

He shrugged. "I'm not so young that I need to prove I'm a man, and I'm not old enough yet that I need to prove I've still got it."

"True enough, I suppose. Do you guys do this every year?"

"Yep, on the first run of the new season the day before we open the ski hill. And yes, I *have* gone traditional Scottish in the past." He cracked a smile. "Back when I was young and dumb enough to think I had something to prove."

They reached the top of the mountain and slid off the chair lift, joining his family at the start of the longest run.

"Well, lass, what d'ye think?" Angus asked.

"Definitely the best view in Northstar," Celeste murmured. "Thanks for inviting me to join you all today. It means a lot to me."

"Ah, ye're not with us yet. Sula, love, give the lass her tammie."

Sula pulled a Scottish tam hat from her snow pants' thigh pocket and handed it to Celeste. It was the same tartan as what she and the rest of her family wore, and she smiled warmly as Celeste traded it for her plain knit hat. "Welcome to the family, dear."

"The family?"

"The Northstar Ski Hill family," Ainsley clarified.

Angus lifted a ski pole and bellowed, "Fàilte!" His

voice echoed down the mountainside, and as soon as it died away, he was off, zigging and zagging through perfect, sparkling powder with a grace that seemed impossible for someone of his size. Sula followed, uttering the same, and then Ainsley. Brodie hung back with Celeste.

"Fall-cha?" she asked him.

"Cheers," he replied. "You're sure you don't mind wasting precious work time helping us toast the new ski season?"

"Why the hell would I mind? Believe me, Brodie, I was not merely being polite when I thanked you and your family for inviting me. Maybe I *should* be working right now, but this is a much better way to spend my afternoon."

In fact, she admitted to herself, she needed this. All of it. Pristine powder, gleaming blue skies, and the charming and invigorating company of a handsome Scotsman and his equally charming family. Maybe she was being rash for getting involved with a new man so soon after Marc's death, but she would *not* worry about that. She'd been trapped in a cage of numb worry for long enough, and this healing warmth was too precious to ignore.

With a wink, Brodie set off after his parents and sister, and Celeste hesitated only a moment longer before following.

A few hours later, Brodie had to leave to go get Brendan from school, and while he was gone, Celeste skied with his family. They barely knew her, but that didn't stop them from folding her into their group as if they'd known her for years. By the time Brodie returned with his son, not a single trace of her earlier anxiety remained.

I am so glad I didn't say no to this.

The fresh, crisp air on her face, the cushy snow beneath her skis, the exertion, and most of all the sense that she was welcome here felt incredible.

* * *

The first three days of the ski hill being open had been more hectic than anyone had expected, a clear sign that the Dunns weren't the only ones excited about this winter's unusually high snowfall. Brodie hadn't had much chance to breathe at work, so the last thing he should want to do was strap on skis again, but it was such a perfect night that he couldn't resist, and he now found himself gliding up the road to the A-frame and the pretty brunette currently calling it home. Being Saturday, Brendan was in Butte with Steph and Russ, and Brodie didn't feel like sitting alone in his house. Even if Celeste didn't feel like a starlit cross-country ski, he might be able to persuade her to let him stay a while.

He leaned his skis against the wall beside the outer door and knocked on the off chance she was in the mudroom. Silence answered his knock, and he remembered that the doorbell didn't work, so he let himself in to the mudroom, knocked on the inner door, and waited. Still no answer, but her truck was parked outside, and he could hear music—loud enough that she probably couldn't hear him knocking. So unless she was out for a walk, which he doubted, she must be home. Cautiously, he opened the door and peeked inside. He spotted her sitting at her computer, but he was too far away to see what she was so absorbed by. Work, no doubt. The Spice Girls belted out an upbeat dance tune, and Brodie stepped further into the house.

She sat with her hands in her lap, her graphics tablet and stylus ignored on her desk, and stared blankly at the computer screen. As he edged closer, he was able to see some of what she was working on—a dark thriller or mystery book cover with a knife gripped tightly in a woman's slender hand and the beginnings of what would eventually be blood dripping off the blade's tip. Even unfinished, the image was shadowy and disturbing with the emphasis clearly on the knife.

The song changed to a tune he recognized from the *Braveheart* soundtrack, and he took another few steps into the cabin to lean against the island, knocking on the stool to announce his presence. Still, she didn't hear it, so he remarked, "I've always been a sucker for bagpipes."

Celeste let out an inhuman scream, and a notebook that had been sitting out of his line of sight in her lap and her chair were sent flying as she scrambled into the far corner of the room in an instinctual, terrified flight. She slid to the floor with her back to the corner, drawing her knees up so that her shins shielded most of her body. Her eyes darted like a cornered animal's, and she didn't seem to recognize him when he padded into the living room with the same carefully placed steps he might use tracking a doe.

"Hey, lass," he cooed. "It's Brodie. I didn't mean to scare you."

If she heard him, she didn't show any sign. The way she hid her face behind her knees and let out panted whimpers broke his heart. This girl had been hurt. Bad. Cruelly, he suspected. He couldn't imagine any sane person reacting like this—retreating deep into herself, locked in a primordial state of fight or flight. Her cat slunk into the living room and went directly to her with his belly low to the ground. He snuck in close to her side, eying Brodie warily with those keen blue eyes.

"I'm not going to hurt her, Bard," Brodie murmured, squatting a few feet away from the woman and her guardian. "Though I'd say someone has, and I'll bet you were around to see it. Wanna tell me what happened, pretty boy?"

The panic had subsided, and Celeste now tipped her head back with her eyes closed. Tears seeped silently from beneath her lashes.

"Celeste?" he asked gently.

"I'm sorry, Brodie," she whispered in response.

So she'd regained enough wits to recognize him. He let out the breath he'd been holding. "No, I'm sorry. I didn't mean to scare the hell out of you, lass. I knocked several times, but I guess you couldn't hear me over your music."

She shook her head.

"Are you going to be all right?"

At last, she opened her eyes, and when she met his gaze, he inhaled sharply. He'd never seen a soul so raw as hers, not even in those first few days after Inez's death when he'd looked at his mother or his own reflection.

"Every time I begin to think I will be… I fall apart again."

"Don't chide yourself for that, lass. Falling apart is part of healing. We fall to pieces so we can build ourselves anew, because sometimes the pain changes us so much that we can't ever again be who we were before." He opened his mouth to say something else, then closed it. What could he say to reassure her when he didn't know what exactly had done this to her?

She crawled over to him, so he sat where he was and pulled her into his arms, perching her on one thigh with her legs in his lap and her arms hooked around his waist. It struck him how easily she fit into him—so tiny, and at the moment, frighteningly fragile. He was under no delusions about her strength and stubborn self-reliance; she was the kind to keep things to herself as best she could until she trusted someone, and the fact that she was letting him see her so vulnerable after just two dates and knowing him for only three weeks made him wonder just how far this thing between them—whatever it was—would go.

Bard nudged and pushed his way into the narrow space between their bodies and tilted his face up with his eyes narrowed in contentment. Brodie took the feline's approval of how he was handling the situation as a compliment, too, and lavished the cat with pets.

"Has anyone ever told you that you purr like a Mack truck, lad?" he asked quietly.

"I tell him all the time that he purrs loud enough to make a diesel jealous," Celeste remarked. "Pretty much the same thing, so I'm sure he knows."

"He's very empathetic for a cat."

She nodded. "He and I have been through a lot together, and there've been times when we've only had each other."

"Bard the Dragonslayer." Brodie wondered again what metaphorical dragons the cat kept at bay but didn't think now was the time to ask. She might trust him enough to show him this side of her, but that didn't mean she'd reached the point that she could talk about what had happened. So, he said, "Let's move to the couch, shall we, and get comfortable."

"You don't have to stay."

"And what if I want to? Because I do, unless you want me to go."

"No.... Stay. Please."

She let go of him only long enough to follow him to the couch, and as soon as he was settled, she promptly tucked herself into his side again. Bard returned to his spot, wedging himself in and purring as loudly as ever. Brodie chuckled fondly.

"Yeah, Binx and Moon are going to be pissed at me again," he murmured. "I'm cheating on them with another cat. How dare I."

"Do they get jealous?"

"Horribly so, but neither of them come from good places, and they don't like to share their spoiling."

"Can't blame them."

"Feeling a little steadier now?"

"Yes. Thank you." She sighed. "I'm tired of this."

"Of what? Turning into a wailing banshee when someone startles you? Or a siren hell-bent on drowning her anger, herself, and the helpless sailor she has her eye on in sex?"

She laughed softly at his quip, once again surprising him. "Both, and a few other things." She tipped her face up, frowning lightly. "Why are you here? I'm pretty sure you didn't come with the intent to scare me—you like to joke around, but you're not mean about it."

"It's a nice night to take in the stars on a pair of cross-country skis, and I thought you might like to join me. But now that I've scared the life out of you, I completely understand if you're not feeling up to it."

"I'm not. Sorry."

"My fault."

"No, it's not. None of this is your fault. If anything, I owe you a lot for your friendship and how much it's helped me already. You have a surprisingly powerful calming effect on me."

"So it would seem."

"What are we doing?"

Frowning, he pulled his head back so he could see her face. She regarded him with a contemplative light in her rich eyes. "What do you mean?"

"I mean, are we friends investigating the possibility of adding benefits, or are we looking for something more serious, more involved?"

"Why don't you tell me? My heartbreaks have been healed a long time now, but yours are barely scabbed over. That is, if they aren't still bleeding. I'm definitely interested in something more serious." He paused for a moment, then added lightly with a twist of his lips, "Despite your volatile moods."

She snorted. "Volatile's about right. But I suppose that's better than what I've been living the last few months. Volatile means I'm feeling *something* again." Sighing, she snuggled closer. "It's probably way too soon, but I want to see how this plays out."

"How long's it been, lass?"

"Marc died on the thirty-first of August, so he's been gone almost three months now."

Died? Brodie tried not to react to that piece of information. "Only three months? Well, hell, you're doing pretty damned good."

"Sure doesn't feel like it."

"Maybe not, but even Brendan's noticed a change in you since the first time he met you."

"He has?"

"After we left the ski-hill Wednesday evening, he told me you don't seem as sad as you did then."

"It's hard to be sad around such a charming little boy… or his equally charming father."

There it was. She'd turned another corner, leaving her fright completely behind her. Pride warmed his heart, and he tightened his arms around her. The mention of his son reminded him that he missed the little boy, and at once, he wished Brendan were here. The kid was such a major part of his life that it felt wrong to separate him from the time he spent with Celeste. She wasn't the only one beginning to trust; after such a short time, Brodie was already beginning to trust her as well. Despite the traumas she'd experienced and her resulting instability, she had a strong, kind heart. This was only temporary, and when she overcame it, he was certain she'd be the kind of woman he'd always envisioned as the mother of his children—capable, compassionate, selfless. The evidence so far pointed to a giant heap of potential for a long term relationship, maybe even to-the-grave long term, but if the novelty of this heady connection between them wore off, he believed she'd do everything in her power to spare his son from the pain of their breakup. *That's* what had been lacking in his previous relationships, and it inspired in him a desire to take a chance.

"As it seems we're both on the same page, shall we agree to pursue this a little more seriously than a date here or there?"

"*Shall we agree?*" She laughed louder this time. "My,

aren't we eloquent this evening?"

"Hey, I know how to use big words. I simply choose to save them for special occasions."

"And this is a special occasion?"

"I believe it is."

"I think you're right. And yes, I do want to explore this more seriously than we have to this point. I may have to ignore the way I feel like I'm using you to pull myself up, but I will because I'm curious… and because I have hope for the first time in months."

"Hope for what?"

"That I'll find a way to rebuild myself. Hopefully as a stronger version." Abruptly, she sat up. "So, how about that trek?"

"I thought you weren't up for it."

"I wasn't, but I am now."

"All right, then. Grab your gear, and I'll meet you outside."

Brodie lavished Bard with a few more pets before he headed outside to click his ski boots back into his skis. Celeste joined him an impressively short time later with her ski pants, boots, and parka on, the tam hat her parents had given her on her head, thick Columbia mittens on her hands, and her skis and poles in her hand. Yet more proof that this girl wasn't a stranger to snow sports, and even more captivating than her quality gear and her efficiency at getting ready was the sincere gleam of anticipation brightening her eyes. He searched for any indication that she was merely hiding the darker thoughts and emotions his unexpected visit had triggered but found nothing. It was as if she hadn't been curled in a ball in the corner just a short time ago, which meant she was either the most gifted actress he'd ever met—doubtful, because that was Shannon's area of expertise; Celeste was honest to the point of terseness—or incredibly resilient.

All evidence weighed, he went with resilient.

While he'd been distracted by her, she'd snapped her boots into her skis, looped the pole tethers around her wrists, and now looked at him expectantly.

"Where to, good sir?"

"There's a trail at the end of this road that heads behind the Bedspread to the road my parents' spread is on. Are you in the mood to meet a few of my family's hairier companions?"

"Uh… that depends. What are we talking about here? Your dad's brother from Scotland? Because that's the only thing coming to mind that might be hairier than you or your dad."

"Excuse me," Brodie gasped in mock offense, "I am *not* hairy."

"Tell that to the thing taking over your face."

Her eyes twinkled merrily, and he chuckled. "You may have a point. But believe me, the ladies and gentlemen I want to introduce you to make me look as hairless as Brendan when he was born."

"Okay. Now I'm *really* curious. *What* are they?"

"Scottish Highland cattle in full winter coats."

"They're supposed to be really docile, aren't they?"

"They are indeed, like giant dogs but with long horns. I'm surprised you know that. Not too many people know much about the breed. At least, not in the States."

"I did a report on Scotland back in high school."

"So, is that a yes to heading over to my folks' place?"

"How far is it?"

"A little under a mile each way. You up for that?"

"Lead the way."

Brodie set off on the trail, which had filled in some since he'd traversed it on Thursday, and Celeste followed close on his heels. He set a leisurely pace so they could enjoy the star-studded beauty of the night, but Celeste was having none of it.

"Come on, slow poke! I'm going to freeze into an icicle back here if we don't pick up the pace. Let's get our blood pumping."

He slid to a stop, then started to turn around on the trail.

"What are you doing?"

"You said you wanted to get your blood pumping, and the best way to do that is back at your cabin. Or mine, if you'd prefer."

"Seriously? Let's turn back then. I can meet your parents' Highlands some other day."

Mischief glittered in her eyes, but at the same time, there was a shadow beside it. She was aware that sex tonight, as cathartic as it might be, wasn't a good idea. But he liked that she was able to joke about it.

Chuckling, he pointed his skis forward again and started off. "Come on."

Trouble. Just as he'd thought the night he'd met her, and he was already mired in it and sinking deeper with each passing day. *Good thing it's the kind of trouble I want to be in.*

Six

"WAS IT RASH TO GIVE UP the Kingston rental?" Celeste asked Shannon. She sat on the couch in her friend's small house on the Bar E Ranch, sipping a steaming mug of after-dinner hot chocolate garnished with a candy cane. Out the big, square window directly ahead of her, a bright smudge of goldenrod across the southeastern sky signaled the last hurrah of day's demise.

"Well, since you extended your stay in the A-frame another month, I'd say it isn't rash at all. It's logical, and it'll save you, what, eight hundred bucks?"

"Sixteen hundred. Gracie had someone waiting for the house, and they're already moving in, so I don't have to pay December's rent."

"That's fantastic, Celeste!"

She smiled. "It kinda is. You guys don't mind me

hanging around until the end of January, do you?"

"I'm *thrilled* you'll be here." Shannon leaned her head on Celeste's shoulders. "I've missed you a lot these last couple years, and it wouldn't hurt my feelings if you decided to move here permanently. Hint hint."

Celeste laughed softly. "It is so *very* tempting."

"That wouldn't have anything to do with Brodie, would it?"

"No, but he's a definite bonus." Exhaling contentedly, she took another sip of her hot chocolate. Thinking of what Brodie had said about the pain sometimes making it impossible to ever again be who they were before it, she smiled. "I'm not back to myself yet, and I may never again be the me I was before… but I might end up a better, reworked version of myself."

"That's a powerful sentiment."

"It's Brodie's, and I've been thinking about it a lot since he said it last Saturday. I don't have to try to put the old me back together, and maybe it sounds strange, but that's kind of a relief. I'm *not* who I was anymore."

"How can you be after that?" Shannon murmured. "I'm sorry I've been so pushy. I just hate to see you hurting."

"I know you do, and I'm sorry I've been such a bitch to you. I appreciate everything you've done for me, and I don't know where I'd be without you."

Shannon shifted on the couch to face Celeste with a mischievous gleam in her warm hazel eyes. "Yeah… I don't think I'm the one who's helped you. Brodie seems to have been a *far* greater influence."

"Maybe so, and maybe that's the way it needs to be.

It's not the women in my life who've hurt me, so it makes sense that it wouldn't be the women I need to help me pick up the pieces and re-forge myself—that part of me never broke." Celeste laughed again. "You know, for being such a joker, he's pretty wise."

"Yes, he is. He could give June a run for her money, that's for sure." Shannon tipped her head against the back of the couch with her face still turned toward Celeste. "It's good to hear you laugh again."

"It *feels* good to laugh again."

Crying from the bedroom drove Shannon off the couch. Celeste folded her arms on the back and watched her friend's departure with a mixture of longing and anxiety. She'd been honest when she'd told Brodie she'd once thought she'd have two or three kids, and part of her wanted them, but whether she would—whether she deserved to have any—was very much up in the air. It was still more difficult to be around Jack than it should be, but interestingly, that did not extend to Brodie's adorable little boy, perhaps because of their ages. Brendan, being well past the baby years, didn't trigger the same angst the infant did.

She had planned to stay until bedtime, but feeling herself closing up again after a delightful evening, Celeste decided it was time to call it a night. When Shannon returned a few minutes later with her young son in her arms, Celeste stood.

"I think I'm going to head home a little earlier than planned. Let you guys have some family time and maybe get a little work done."

"Please don't go," Shannon said. "We're having a great time."

"We are, and I think I'd rather end it on a high note."

Shannon glanced at her son, then back at Celeste with a sympathetic smile. "I was hoping that might be getting a little easier for you, too."

"Not yet. But I'm hopeful."

Celeste briefly embraced her friend, then headed to the front door to don her parka, hat, and gloves. The door opened, and Ty entered in a whirlwind of icy air. He'd left them briefly to check on a horse that had come up lame this morning.

"You can't be heading home already," he said. "The fun's just beginning."

"Sorry, Ty, but I'm fast approaching my limit, and I don't want to push it and ruin the evening."

"Understandable. Thanks for coming over, Celeste. It's been great having you in Northstar, and I'm glad you've decided to extend your stay."

"You're sweet. A liar, but sweet. And I'm working on making your sentiments the truth."

"I'm not a liar, and I know you are. Would tomorrow be too soon to get together again?" Ty glanced at his wife and grinned. "We're going to cut our Christmas tree tomorrow, and if you come with us, you can get one for your cabin, too."

"Thanks, but I don't think I'll be putting up a tree this year. It's great being here with you guys, and believe me, it helps *a lot*, but I'm not feeling very Christmassy."

"You've been through a lot this year. A lot in the last few months. So, how about you come down for dinner after we get back? And maybe you'd like to invite Brodie and Brendan to come with you?"

"I don't know how ready Brodie is for me to be spending that amount of time with his son just yet, but he said…." She stopped herself short of expressing the doubt that surged and smiled. "That'd be wonderful, Ty. Thank you. I'll ask him. G'night, you three."

Celeste stepped out the door and exhaled. Leaving was the right decision. She'd genuinely enjoyed herself this evening and for the longest stretch of time yet without incident, but her reserve of energy was running low, and she needed some quiet time alone to recharge. She climbed in her borrowed truck and drove home to her A-frame without fear. Just like everything else, she'd gotten used to it. She'd get used to being around Jack, too, in time. And maybe someday she'd forgive herself.

As she drove out of the trees on Lightning Ridge Road and Brodie's house just beyond came into view, she spotted him sitting on the bench in his yard with his hands in his coat pockets and his gaze turned toward the stars. He didn't seem to notice her approach, or if he did, he didn't acknowledge it. Figuring it was a degree or two below zero, she turned down his driveway, parked beside his truck, and left the engine running. She stepped out into the frigid night with the corners of her mouth upturned.

"I've never tried a Brodie-cicle before. Are they tasty?"

He met her gaze, but when he smiled, there was no trace of his usual mirth. "Hello, Celeste. Fancy meeting you right here, right now, on this day."

"Seeing as I'm staying just up the road from you, I'd say it's more a probability than a rare coincidence."

"Even more intriguing."

"Something up?"

"Yeah," he replied in the same thoughtful tone, turning his gaze skyward again. "The stars."

She glanced at the glittering tapestry above them, then looked at him again with her brows lifted in inquiry. "You seem to have quite a fascination with them."

"I do. Thirteen years ago today, I made a promise to my sister under the stars that I would always remember to find the joy in life and to never let anyone or anything hurting suffer alone."

Celeste did the math in her head, and it seemed like an odd conversation for Brodie to have with Ainsley, who would've been a preteen thirteen years ago. "You have another sister?"

"Half-sister. Inez. She was one of the most beautiful souls I've ever known. Physically, she was gorgeous—very much her Spanish father's daughter with long dark hair, dark eyes, exotic—but it was her heart that made her truly breathtaking. Have you seen that thing going around the Internet about how we're put on this earth to learn how to be good souls and that dogs live such comparatively short lives because they are already good souls?"

"I have. It's one of my favorites."

"That was Inez. She had this innate *goodness*, and she knew how to enjoy every moment of life. I'm sure she got angry or cried, but I don't remember that. I remember only her light."

It was clear that Inez was no longer with him, and her curiosity scuffled with her respect of his privacy, but after a moment, the former won. "Brodie…? What happened to her?"

"She died."

It was the answer she'd expected, if more vague, but Celeste folded her arms tightly across her chest, hugging herself as much to ward off the surge of grief for his loss as to fend off the cold. "How?"

"Leukemia. She'd *just* landed a big-time modeling contract, and it was at her first shoot that she began to feel like something wasn't right. It happened so fast, and yet, the waiting and the not knowing felt like a dozen lifetimes stretched out one after the other. The doctors said a bone marrow transplant might save her, and I turned out to be a good match, but it wasn't enough. She was too far gone by then. Just twenty-one years old with so much promise. She was my best friend. I drove her home from the hospital, and when we got home, we just sat in my truck and talked while we stargazed. She died just before sunrise as the last stars faded from the sky."

It was an old pain, one he had long since woven into the fabric of himself, and he revealed it with a level if quiet voice, waxing almost poetical in tone, but Celeste felt compelled to sidle over to him and tuck her arms around him in a silent show of support even though he probably didn't *need* it. He locked his arms around her and squeezed her tight for a moment before relaxing with his cheek resting atop her head.

"I'm sorry, Brodie," she whispered. "The way you describe her, even if you hadn't called her beautiful, I would've known she was. I hope she knew how lucky she was to be loved so deeply by her brother."

"She knew."

"That's how you figured it out."

"Figured what out?"

"That sometimes pain changes us so much we can't be who we were before."

He nodded, again gazing at the stars. "I'd like to think I'm a better me than I was before. I certainly ditched the impatience and learned how to appreciate even the smallest details. Like how the stars sparkle more on a cold winter's night than in summertime when the air is thicker with humidity. And the secretiveness in my son's voice ten minutes ago when he kicked me out of the house so he could wrap the present he made for me at Stephanie's this weekend."

"Brendan's here?" Celeste asked, a little surprised the boy was unattended inside. Figuring Brodie knew *way* more about what was appropriate or allowable for an almost-six-year-old boy than she did, she chided herself for the jab of censure. "Why didn't he wrap it at his mom's?"

"She hasn't bought any wrapping paper yet, and I get the impression that making whatever he made was sort of a last-minute idea. He's prone to those, just like he's prone to asking a million questions."

"Cute. Spontaneity, creativity, and inquisitiveness are good traits to have."

"Yes, they are." Turning his attention fully to her, he asked, "You want to come in for a little while? He should be done wrapping by now, and if he isn't, maybe you could give him a hand? I would, but I'm not allowed to see."

"I'd love to."

She shut her truck down, then followed him into his cabin. Just inside the arctic entry, two Labrador retrievers waited to greet them with bodies wiggling in excitement.

Celeste didn't immediately return their greeting, shocked to see them *right there*. He'd said more than once that he had dogs, and she even remembered their names—Jake and Charlie—and she felt silly for her surprise.

"Don't tell me you don't like dogs," Brodie remarked, eyeing her. "Not liking dogs is a deal breaker for me."

His tone was joking and light, as usual, but she didn't doubt he meant what he said.

"You said not liking *animals* was a deal breaker, not specifically dogs. But don't worry. I like dogs. I always wanted one, but I've never lived in a place where I could have one, so I don't have much experience with them."

"Dogs are easy. Lavish them with pets, and they'll love you forever."

"I don't know why they surprised me," she murmured, leaning down to do as he instructed. "Hey, guys. Charlie's the black Lab, right? And Jake's the yellow?"

"Yep."

Jake had no qualms whatsoever about throwing himself at Celeste, but Charlie, as enthusiastically as she'd greeted Brodie, was hesitant. She stood a couple feet away, sniffing and wagging her tail more slowly than her companion.

"It's okay, pretty girl. I didn't mean to offend you." Celeste looked to Brodie. "What'd I do wrong?"

"Nothing. Charlie's just a little wary. She came from an abusive, neglectful home, so it takes her a few minutes longer than Jake to warm up to new people."

Celeste dropped to one knee, held her hand out, and waited for Charlie to make the next move. When the dog stepped closer and wagged her tail a little faster, Celeste whispered, "I understand, sweetheart. But you have a good home now, don't you, and all that is behind you."

Kind brown eyes met hers, and the connection of two kindred souls sent a shock through Celeste. With a soft whine, Charlie scooted close to her and sat. Celeste obligingly stroked her hand over the dog's head and down her neck and back. Jake tilted his head, tongue lolling out one side of his mouth and a light of curiosity in his eyes.

"Well, now, looks like you have a new friend for life," Brodie remarked gently. "Come on inside."

"Why were the dogs out here instead of outside with you or inside with Brendan?"

"Their paws were getting cold, but if I'd let them in the house with Brendan, they'd've been right in the middle of his wrapping job trying to help."

"Ah. I didn't think they'd be anything but spoiled rotten house dogs by the way you've talked about them."

"Of course they are."

They kicked their boots off and shrugged out of their coats in the arctic entry, and when Celeste followed Brodie into the main house, a waft of warm air spiced with the mouthwatering aroma of freshly baked cookies greeted her. With that scent filling her lungs, the dry, soothing heat of a wood fire, and the cozy golden wood tones of the logs, it felt immediately like home. The structure, like many in Northstar, was log, L-shaped with a fairly steep pitch to the roof, and like her A-frame, it had a loft over the back half of the house and a cathedral ceiling over the front half.

To her right was the well-lit, spacious kitchen, and to the left was a full dining room. To the right side of the kitchen was a hallway that led to the main bathroom and a guest bedroom Brodie used as an office. A wide living area with big windows—occupied by an obviously frustrated Brendan—took up the front of the house with stairs on the left wall leading up to the loft. The source of the soothing heat was a big stone fireplace directly across from the stairs.

A towering tree stood at the center of the far wall in the living room, but it and the rest of the house were only partially decorated, and that work-in-progress air only added to the coziness of home. This house was *lived in.*

"Wow, Brodie," Celeste breathed, absently stroking Charlie's head. "This is beautiful."

"The master bedroom is right above us in the loft, and Brendan's bedroom and a three-quarter bath are above the guest room and downstairs bathroom."

Brodie was careful to keep his voice low, but it wasn't quiet enough; Brendan's head snapped up, and his red-eyed scowl of frustration shifted into one of disappointment as he scrambled to cover up his gift with the pile of shredded and crumpled wrapping paper. "Papa! You're not s'posed to see!"

"I know, lad. Celeste stopped by while I was waiting outside, and she and I thought you might need a little assistance."

The frown vanished. "Really? You want to help me, Celeste?"

"Sure. If your dad doesn't mind leaving us alone for a bit…." She looked uncertainly to Brodie, whose expression was one of mild amusement. There was no trace of concern, but until he said he was okay with his son being alone with her, the quiver of uncertainty would remain.

"We'll come get you as soon as we're done."

"Can she help, Papa?"

"You want me to go back outside? How am I supposed to peek?"

"You *aren't* s'posed to," Brendan retorted. "That's why you gotta go back outside—so you *can't* peek."

"Are you sure I won't be able to see in the windows?"

"Papa!"

Chuckling, Brodie surprised both his son and Celeste when he leaned over and kissed her cheek and then trotted out to the arctic entry with Jake on his heels. He held the door open and waited a moment for Charlie to join him, but she stayed beside Celeste, so he shrugged and closed the door. Celeste stared after him for a moment, and when she finally pulled her wits together enough to turn her attention to the little boy she was now alone with, she found him staring at the closed door with his mouth open.

"What?" Celeste asked, concerned.

"He's never kissed anyone in front of me before. Not even on the cheek. I mean, other than Aunt Ainsley or Nana and Granddad, but they don't count. It's different."

"He hasn't?"

Brendan nodded, frowning, and she couldn't tell if he approved or not. Or maybe he just didn't know her well enough to decide if he *should* approve. It wasn't something she needed to dwell on, so she joined him on the floor with Charlie flopped beside them and asked to see the gift. It was a picture frame decorated with stickers of skis, snowboards, snowshoes, and snowmobiles with a photo of him and his dad making goofy faces. She recognized the top of the ski lift in the background.

"I didn't do as good a job as I wanted to," Brendan murmured.

When he sniffed, she realized his eyes were red because he'd been crying. Poor guy. Instinctively, she wanted to hug him and tell him that it was okay to be frustrated when things didn't work the way he wanted and that he'd learn how to wrap a package on his own and that he shouldn't let it get him down. But it wasn't her place, so she subdued the instinct and maintained her silence.

"I saw a frame like that at the store with Mom and Russ," the boy continued quietly, "but the skis and stuff were carved into it, and Mom took me back to buy it, but it was gone. She said I should try to make one, but it's not very good."

"Oh, honey, it's beautiful, and I know your dad will love it even more than he would have the store-bought one. Wanna know why?"

Brendan regarded her with a doubtful expression.

"Because you made it. And that means there's more love in it. It takes love to make things like this because they take time to make, and time is precious—something you can't buy and can't get back once it's gone." Realizing he probably wouldn't understand most of what she'd said, Celeste snapped her mouth closed. "Let's get it wrapped so we can call your dad back in. We don't want him to freeze out there, do we?"

"No. Um, Celeste?"

"Hmm?"

"There isn't enough wrapping paper left. I kinda messed it all up."

"Not a problem. We can either tape it together, or....

I have an idea. Do you have any brown paper bags? Like paper grocery sacks?"

"Yeah. Papa keeps them over beside the trash can."

"How about twine?"

"What's twine?"

"That kind of rough, tan-colored string."

"Oh! Yeah, we have that, too."

He bounced up and raced into the kitchen. He snatched a paper sack from beside the trash can and pulled a ball of twine out of one of the drawers nearby, then raced back into the living room and looked at her expectantly. She showed him how to cut the paper bag and trim it to the right size to wrap the frame without having too much extra and asked him to tape it in place as she folded it. Then she cut a length of twine and twisted and tied it around the package, finishing it off with a simple bow.

"It's a lot easier with two people, isn't it?" she asked.

"Yeah."

Handing the package to Brendan, she said, "There you go. If you want to make it prettier and more Christmassy, here's what you do. Look through those boxes of Christmas stuff and see if you can find some little things to add to it, like a pinecone or a piece of fake holly or a small ornament. Something like that. And then we'll tie or tape whatever you find to the present."

"What if I can't find anything?"

"Then get your crayons or markers and draw something on the paper. Make it your own wrapping paper."

"Okay!"

He didn't find anything to use in the boxes that

wasn't attached to something, but within minutes, he had covered the dining room table with art supplies and was busily covering the plain brown paper with wobbly holly leaves and berries, Christmas trees, and snowflakes. With his lack of practice, his artwork was understandably uneven and imperfect, but the love and effort he put into it made his present among the most beautiful pieces of art.

"Mind if I let your dad in? He and I can sit on the couch while you work here at the table."

"Uh-huh," Brendan agreed, too busy with his task to form a more articulate response.

Without thinking what she was doing, she affectionately ruffled his hair as she walked by him toward the door to get Brodie. Just as she stepped away, she heard the door hinges creak and glanced up to see Brodie pop his head inside. There was no way he hadn't seen her gesture, and at once, she realized what she'd done and stopped dead in her tracks.

"Can I come in yet?" he asked.

"Uh...." Her mouth went dry, and nervousness quivered.

"It's not a complex question. I just need a simple yes or no."

"Yes." She shook herself out of her shock. "The present is wrapped, but you'll have to join me in the living room because he's adding a little something extra special to the wrapping job."

Forcing the lingering flutter of nerves into submission, she strode forward and took Brodie's hand, then dragged him quickly to the living room. They flopped together with a glorious lack of pretense onto the plush couch, sinking deep into its cushions and falling together in laughter. Both dogs sprawled below them. Still chuckling, Brodie took her by the chin and kissed her soundly.

Breathless and wide-eyed, she met his gaze head on. "Wh-what was that for?"

"We *did* agree we wanted to take this further and see where it goes, did we not?"

"We did."

"Well, that's what I'm doing."

"Maybe I should ask what all *taking it further* entails."

"Dinners and lunches and, down the road, maybe even a few breakfasts together, starlight strolls, spoiling my son, hugs and kisses, and… snuggling on the couch together."

"Is that all?" she asked softly.

He responded by tucking his arms around her and pulling her close. She sighed contentedly and caught herself. It was so easy and natural to be with him, but after her experiences with Marc, shouldn't she be more wary? She'd been blind to the darkness in him. Was it possible she might miss it again?

Glancing over her shoulder at the little boy still diligently decorating his father's Christmas present, she shook her head. There wasn't a hint of darkness in Brodie; if there were, it would be a shadow over his son, and that boy gleamed brighter than the sun.

To divert her attention, she shifted her gaze to the half-decorated tree and the boxes of Christmas decorations. "I was so sure I didn't want to decorate my A-frame for Christmas, but now that I see what you and Brendan have already done here, I kinda want to. I'm supposed to head over to Ty and Shannon's for dinner again tomorrow, but I want to have them and you and Brendan over to my place for dinner instead." She tilted her head and turned her eyes on Brodie, who observed her with a faint, contented smile softening his features. "I can't believe I'm saying this, but I'd love to have you all help me decorate."

"Why can't you believe you're saying it?"

"Because…." She closed her mouth, frowning. Could she admit it? Firming her resolve, she said, "Because I haven't wanted to decorate my space with *anything* let alone decorate for the holidays. But now I do. Will you help me do that?"

"I can't imagine anything more fun or a better way to peel back a few more of your layers."

"Layers? I'm not a complicated person, Brodie. I love art, I love the snow and the outdoors, and I love the beauty of simple things." *And I think I'm starting to love you, too.*

"Oh, I agree that in some ways you're a very simple person. But in others, you are *definitely* complex."

"Like how?"

He shook his head. "Nope. Not gonna tell you tonight. Tonight's for focusing on the light. I don't talk about shadowy things on the anniversary of my sister's last night of life."

Celeste held her hands up, conceding. "All right, let's talk about Christmas trees. Ty offered to let me cut one off his ranch, and I'm thinking… maybe we can make an evening of it, the six of us." Reining in the sudden and delicious excitement, she sighed. "I'm being selfish. You still have to finish decorating here, and Ty and Shannon will want to decorate their—"

"Don't do that, Celeste. We're all your friends, and you are important to us. To Shannon and Ty, and more and more the longer I know you, to me as well. Besides, I'm sure Brendan would love it."

"Are you… okay with me being around him now?"

"I am. For one, he likes you. For another, *I* like you. For a third, you have something special about you that makes me think you'll make a great mom someday—a patience and a simple enjoyment of the silly things young kids enjoy."

Celeste lowered her gaze and tried not to wince. One day not so long ago, she'd hoped she'd be a good mother some day, but now…. Now she wasn't sure she'd ever recover the heart to find out.

"Speaking of trees and the things that go under it, what's my present?" he asked.

He said it loudly enough that she knew he meant his son to hear. Was he giving her a chance to prove she wouldn't betray Brendan's trust? And had he sensed the turn of her mood and was now trying to redirect her? Both, she decided, noting the way he leveled his gaze on her with one corner of his lips lifted.

"Uh-uh, mister," she replied with more playfulness than she would've thought possible with those memories threatening. "My lips are sealed. How're you doing over there, Brendan?"

"Good!" the boy replied brightly.

Celeste snuggled into Brodie's side, slipping her arms around him, and was grateful for his calming presence. On the one hand, the idea of stepping out of her cocoon of cold emptiness to embrace life again terrified her. On the other, she hungered for the laughter and love and holiday cheer that was certain to saturate tomorrow as she and her friends actively filled the hollowness within her.

Suddenly, she noticed the two cats stalking toward the couch, one white, one black. The white one—Moon, she recalled—had no tail.

"I was beginning to wonder where your cats were," she said quietly so as not to spook the cats.

"They were probably crashed out on my bed upstairs, the lazy bums." He called them over, and like loyal dogs, they obeyed.

In short order, both cats were curled up with Celeste and Brodie, purring loudly—though not as loudly as Bard—and kneading the couch cushions in their pleasure as both humans showered them with attention. A beautiful little boy and four pets who obviously thought Brodie was their benevolent king, an uncanny way of knowing what to say or do to soothe her, and a lighthearted sense of humor that could make her smile even when she didn't want to…. As far as she could tell, the man was a genuine catch.

"I don't care what any of those other women say about you, Brodie," she whispered. "You're pretty amazing."

His only response was to tighten his arms around her, and it was all she needed.

Seven

BRODIE CLOSED THE DOOR of the schoolhouse's mudroom door and stomped the snow from his boots on the coarse mat just inside, then dusted the snowflakes from his coat and hair. Just as he was about to open the main door to pop his head into the single classroom, April Fitzwater pushed it open, and he jerked back so it didn't smack him in the face.

"Hi, Brodie," she greeted. "Sorry about that. Come on in."

"Sorry I'm late. I had a customer at the ski hill who wouldn't let me get away."

"No worries. You're only five minutes late, and Brendan's having fun coloring."

Brendan was at his desk finishing up his coloring sheet of Rudolph the Red-nosed Reindeer. Brodie frowned.

His son's face was pale, and he was breathing through his mouth, sniffing frequently and so loudly that Brodie heard it from several feet away.

"Hey, lad," Brodie said quietly. "You feeling all right? You don't look so good."

"I'm fine, Papa," he replied, glancing up from his paper.

Brodie squatted beside his son's desk and rested the inside of his wrist against Brendan's forehead. The boy was a touch warmer than usual but not feverish. Still, if he was coming down with a cold, they should probably cancel their plans for the evening so he could stay home and rest. Brodie didn't like the idea of calling Celeste and telling her they wouldn't be coming up to help her decorate, but he liked the thought of his son getting sick even less. And today, of all days, he was already too aware of illness in general. Thirteen years ago today, he'd lost his half-sister to leukemia, and unlike last night, when he'd been able to focus only on her life, it was impossible not to think of her death today.

A head cold's nothing to worry about, he reminded himself. *Unless it turns into pneumonia.*

"How long's he been feeling crummy?" Brodie asked April.

"He hasn't been, or I would've called you to come get him. It's a stuffy nose, Brodie."

"And the start of a fever."

"I've already checked his temperature, more than once. He's still within the normal range, and has been all day. He's actually cooler now than he was the first time I checked late this morning." She rested her hand on his shoulder and squeezed. "You're just hyper aware today, and that's perfectly understandable, but Brendan's just fine."

"Even so, I think we should stay home tonight, lad. I'm sure Celeste won't mind."

"But, Papa, I wanna go!"

"We'll talk about it in the car. Finish your work."

Brodie stood and walked out to the arctic entry to grab Brendan's coat and backpack.

"Really, Brodie, he's okay," April said gently. "Frowning like that, you're starting to make me feel like I don't know how to take care of children even though I have four of my own."

He opened his mouth to retort, then snapped it shut, taking the hint. He was overreacting. "I'm sorry, April. I didn't mean to come across like that. You're a great mom and a great teacher, and I know Brendan's in good hands with you. It's just… today."

"I know." She gave him a brief hug. "So, Celeste…."

"What about her?"

"Brendan's been going on about her all day. She's your neighbor, right? Shannon's friend?"

"That's right."

"Brendan says you kissed her last night."

Brodie glanced in his son's direction and scowled. "So?"

"So… this is interesting. The man we were all beginning to think might stay single forever has found someone he likes enough to kiss in front of his son—a someone he's known not quite a month. Which naturally makes it even more interesting, because as I recall, the last woman you dated lasted for three months, and you never once kissed her in front of Brendan. What was her name? Lacy? Kasey? I don't even remember."

"The last one was Lacy. But Kasey before her didn't last even that long."

"But Celeste is different."

"Yeah. She is."

"The whole valley's talking about her. Mostly, I think, because not too many people have even met her let alone spent enough time with her to get to know her." April grinned. "And you know how Northstar is."

"I do. Honestly, she's not the easiest person to know. She keeps a lot close to her heart, and I suspect for a very good reason. But I'm peeling back her layers."

"And I'm guessing you're liking what you're finding as you do."

"That's a fair assumption to make. Like you said, she's different. She's enshrouded in a thunderstorm, but I get the feeling that once the storm tears itself apart, she'll shine like the brightest stars on the clearest night." *Like last night. I saw a true glimpse of that light when she asked about Inez.*

April stared at him, her mouth hanging open. A moment later, she snapped it closed. "Oh, Brodie, you're in trouble. You've got it *bad.*"

He gave a huff of laughter. "I figured I was in trouble the moment I saw her walk out of the Ramshorn's pool house her first night in Northstar."

"And rumor has it she recently extended her stay here another month. Maybe you aren't the only one who has it bad." Ty's sister winked. "This is going to be fun to watch."

"So my sister said that first night. Well, looks like Brendan is finished, so we'll get out of your hair so you can go home before midnight."

Together, they gathered the little boy's things and cleaned up his desk area. The speed with which Brendan donned his boots, coat, hat, and mittens was a testament to how excited he was to see Celeste again… almost as if he was trying to prove that he felt good enough to go to her house. Despite April's reassurances, Brodie didn't like the pallor of his son's face, and as they drove home from the school, he again said he thought it best if they stayed home tonight.

"Papa, no! I'm fine. Really. I want to go. I promise I'll get better."

"Getting better isn't something we can just *do*, Brendan." If it were that simple, Inez would still be alive. "You have to give your body time and rest to fight off whatever's making you sick."

"Please, Papa. I'm okay, and I really want to help Celeste decorate Fred's cabin."

"I know you do, but if you're getting—"

"*Papa*… I'm *fine*. You like her, too, don't you? And you want to spend time with her, too, right?"

"Of course I do."

"Do you want to marry her?"

Brodie's head snapped around, and he gaped at his son. "Where on earth did *that* come from?"

"Well, mom started kissing Russ a while ago, and now he wants to marry her, and you kissed Celeste last night…."

"Russ asked your mom to marry him?"

"Not yet, but he told me he was gonna. I was s'posed to tell you last night, but I forgot. Sorry, Papa."

"It's okay, lad." He laughed. "About time he proposed. You all right with that? If your mom marries him, he'll become your stepdad."

"I like Russ. So, if you married Celeste, that'd make her my stepmom, wouldn't it?"

"Yes, it would, but it's way too early to know if that's going to happen, so don't get your hopes up. I know you like her—you've made that *quite* clear—but sometimes, things just don't work out."

"Like you and Mom didn't work out?"

"Exactly." Brodie pressed his wrist to Brendan's forehead again. Already, his son's skin felt cooler. Sighing, he acquiesced. "All right, we'll keep our date with Celeste. But here's the deal. If you start feeling crummy or if Ty and Shannon don't want to take a chance on you getting Jack sick, we go home immediately. Fair enough?"

"Thanks, Papa!"

They stopped at home just long enough to drop off Brendan's backpack, let the dogs out, check the animals' food and water bowls, and grab the box of Christmas tree ornaments and decorations they weren't going to use this year, then drove up to the A-frame. When they arrived, Ty and Shannon's truck was parked by the woodshed, but the one they'd lent Celeste was nowhere in sight. Brodie climbed out of his truck, grabbed the box of decorations, and followed his energetic son to the back door. They knocked, and Ty's voice answered from within, beckoning them in.

Once they had shed their winter wear, they headed inside to find the horse trainer alone inside filling the stand of the tall but narrow spruce with water. Bard sat beside him, patiently waiting for attention.

"Where are the girls and Jack?" Brodie inquired. "I thought Celeste said they'd be back before Brendan got out of school."

"That was the plan, and if they aren't here in ten minutes, I'm going to send out a search party."

"Well, it *is* snowing, and I'm sure Badger Pass is snotty. They're probably just taking it slow."

"That's why I haven't called the sheriff's department. Yet. Hey, Brendan. How are ya, kid?"

"Good."

"Could be better," Brodie corrected. "I think he might be coming down with a cold, so if you don't want Jack exposed, speak now or forever hold your peace."

"Jack's already been exposed. Hunter was sick last week, which is probably where you got it, Brendan."

When Brendan grinned triumphantly at him, Brodie stuck his tongue out at the boy, then headed into the living room to greet Celeste's cat and introduce him to Brendan. Every bit his father's son, Brendan was instantly taken with the large black feline with the bright blue eyes, and the cat seemed as drawn to the boy. Brendan found a cat toy, and the two launched into a game of cat-and-toy-mouse that soon erupted in laughter that had both Brodie and Ty grinning like fools.

"Nothing quite like a child's laughter, is there," Ty remarked quietly.

"There really isn't. Hey, Brendan?"

"Yeah, Papa?"

"Please don't tear up Celeste's house, all right? And make sure you stay away from her desk and work area, okay?

I'm going to step outside and bring some firewood in. Ty, care to join me?"

"Sure."

Celeste had a sizeable stack of split wood, but rather than deplete it, Brodie split some more, and Ty carried the pieces inside. They'd just about finished when the women pulled up in Celeste's borrowed pickup, and Ty's relief was palpable.

"How shitty were the roads?" Brodie asked. "Because Ty was about to send out the National Guard."

"They were ridiculous, but not as ridiculous as the crowds in Devyn," Shannon replied. "It's only the first of December, but apparently everyone suddenly realized that Christmas is just around the corner."

"Did you find everything you needed?"

"And then some," Celeste said, beaming. With a brow lifted, she glanced at Ty's armload of logs and the ax Brodie rested over his shoulder. "There's a whole stack of split logs in the shed."

"I know. Consider this me fulfilling my offer to come over and help you split some, since I never did make it up here to do that."

"Oh, I'd forgotten that."

He cocked his head and studied her with narrowed eyes. "You're in a good mood."

"Yeah," she agreed. "I am. So, I'm going to set aside my stubborn independence and ask you strapping gents to give us a hand with all this junk."

Brodie peered into the back of the pickup, and his mouth fell open as his eyes took in the piles of purchases. "Holy crap, lass. What'd you do, buy the whole store?"

"Close enough. You see, I have all this extra money suddenly, now that I'm not paying rent on my house in Washington, so I decided to splurge on—"

"Wait. What?" His heart jumped like a racehorse at the starting bell. "Just how long are you planning to stay in Northstar?"

Her grin turned shy, and a pretty blush climbed her cheeks. "I don't know yet. I'm taking it one month at a time, but I know I don't want to go back until I've finished rebuilding myself… if I ever go back. I talked to Grandma Letty two days ago, and she thinks I should just stay here, start completely fresh away from… everything."

"Can't say I'm at all disappointed to hear that." He'd meant to say it teasingly, but it came out as a soft entreaty. Aware that they had an audience, he cleared his throat. "I'll, uh, just put the ax back, and then you can tell me where inside you want me to pile everything. That is, of course, if you want me to stick around after you walk in and see my son destroying your house with your cat as an accomplice."

"Let them destroy it. They can't break anything I can't fix or replace, and it's good for Bard to have someone other than me to spoil him."

"You *are* in a good mood."

She laughed and started grabbing bags out of the back of the truck. Brodie set the ax in the woodshed and followed suit, glancing between Ty and Shannon with his brows lifted. They answered with surprised grins of their own and shrugged. Shannon had her hands full with Jack, but Ty helped Brodie grab sacks full of Christmas decorations, groceries, and art supplies including a couple of canvases, mat board, and a couple dozen other crafty items he had no hope of naming. Between them, they were able to carry in more than half of the bags in the truck, and as she passed them on her way back out, Celeste quipped that they were showing off.

"Nah. I just don't want to spend any more time out in the cold than I have to," Ty retorted.

Brodie glanced at the notecard Celeste had tacked to the inside of the interior door's frame. She was definitely saving herself, he mused, wondering if she had yet reached a place that she could see she was. Look how far she'd already come in just the three and a half weeks he'd known her. It'd been days since she'd propositioned him, and he hadn't seen a trace of her to-hell-with-it recklessness last night or yet today. Pride warmed his heart. *That* was how she differed from the other women he'd dated—she had a battle to fight, and she was fighting it. It wasn't that the others didn't have their share of trials, but he doubted one of them had ever experienced anything like what had so damaged Celeste. Her undeniable courage and resilience was attractive.

Maybe that's why I'm so drawn to wounded things—I love to see them come back and win. Because Inez lost.

As if she'd sensed the direction of his thoughts, Celeste met and held his gaze as he set his plethora of sacks on the dining room table. "Are you doing all right today?"

"More or less. Every other day of the year, it's getting easier not to think about her, but today…. It's always tough, even after so many years."

"I'm kinda surprised you didn't want to spend today with your family."

He shrugged. "After Ainsley turned eighteen, we

decided it wasn't doing anyone good to actively note the anniversary of Inez's death. Better to focus on the good."

"Like last night, when you told me you only wanted to focus on the light."

He inhaled deeply and let it out. "That's the theory, but it didn't stop me from freaking out a little bit at Ty's sister because Brendan has a stuffy nose and she didn't call me to come get him."

"Why would she call you for something as minor as a stuffy nose?"

"Exactly."

"I'll bet some peppermint tea would help clear up that stuffiness a bit. May I make some for him?"

"Sure." He almost told her she didn't need to ask his permission to do something nice for his son but stopped short. He noted it, though, more than a little fascinated at the idea that he was already so comfortable with her interactions with his son. "I suppose he'd like that. He loves candy canes and peppermint hot chocolate. Why don't you do that while I bring in more bags?"

He didn't wait for her answer, striding quickly outside. For a moment, he leaned against the truck's tailgate with his arms folded across the top and stared at the house. Ty, who'd beat him back out to the truck, regarded him with a brow lifted but said nothing, only gathered another load of bags and left Brodie to his ponderings. Methodically, Brodie slipped his hands through handles on the bags— canvas, he noted consciously for the first time. Of course they were canvas. A woman who ate neither pork nor beef and only purchased cage-free chicken and organic fruits and vegetables because she was environmentally conscious would never use the plastic, store-provided sacks. His lips twitched. He tried to reduce his footprint, too, but not to the extent she did… and despite the number of times he'd rolled his eyes at people just like her, he found her quiet, unassuming dedication to reducing her impact on the planet both adorable and inspiring.

But Brendan…. That was the most telling revelation of all. He'd never—*never*—felt secure enough with any woman to let his son see any hint of intimacy between him and her, and he'd also never desired a connection between his son and the woman. Steph was the exception, but she was his mother. He'd looked for that indefinable *something* in the women he dated, but he hadn't seen it or hadn't seen enough of it. Until Celeste.

"Hey, Brodie! Did you freeze to the truck?" Shannon called out the door.

"I think I might have."

"Well, hurry up, would ya? Celeste says the box of peppermint tea is in one of the bags you have."

Brodie grabbed the rest of Celeste's purchases out of the back of the truck and headed inside, kicking his boots off in the mudroom on his way through. He expected Brendan to still be playing with Bard, but instead he was helping Celeste, Shannon, and Ty unpack the bags and organize the chaos that had taken over the A-frame's main floor. There were sacks and decorations and groceries everywhere, and in the middle of it was a very smug Bard. Brodie idly wondered if the cat was pleased because he'd soon have all manner of Christmassy things to annihilate, if he liked all the attention he was undoubtedly getting, or if he enjoyed seeing his mistress so happy again. From what he knew of the big cat, all three but in reverse order.

After Brodie deposited the rest of the bags in the space Shannon cleared on the table, he wandered into the living room to watch his son interact with Celeste. She had such a natural camaraderie with the boy, and while Brendan was always quick to help, he was noticeably quicker to please her, wanting her attention. And she was just as happy to give it.

The contents of all the bags were stowed with the exception of the Christmas decorations, and those were placed on the floor near the tree. While Brendan sipped the peppermint tea Celeste had made him—Brodie was mildly surprised he liked it—he and Celeste got started on the cranberry-and-popcorn garland while Shannon and Ty draped clear mini-lights around the spruce. Brodie made himself useful by untangling the hooks for the satiny red glass balls and snooped through the rest of the decorations Celeste had bought, gathering bits and pieces of an impression of what her tree would look like when it was finished. Artsy, like her, and rustic, like Northstar. Delicate stars made of slender willow sticks, glass icicles, the most incredible blown glass spheres with an iridescent sheen of oil that made them look like soap bubbles, burlap bows stamped with red and silver and gold glitter snowflakes…. Was this the new Celeste she was building? A combination of the old pieces of herself she'd deemed too important to throw away and the new pieces she was bringing together with the influence of her temporary—or new?—home? If so, he was in love.

* * *

Stephanie Haigwood was both exactly the kind of

woman Celeste expected Brodie would find attractive and different. She was easy-going with the same quickness to find the humor in any situation that Brodie had—she'd answered the door covered in flour and bits of cookie dough and jokingly called her disheveled appearance the result of a poltergeist taking up residence in her mixer—but where Brodie's life clearly revolved around their son, Stephanie seemed almost awkward with the boy. She obviously loved him, and he loved her in return; it was more the way she looked to Brodie for reassurance when she ran her plans for the weekend by him. Maybe it was merely the fact that Brodie was the custodial parent, but the fact that he was said a lot, too.

"So, you're the woman Brendan has been chattering about non-stop," Stephanie said, perching on the edge of the couch cushion. She gestured for Brodie and Celeste to sit.

Brodie shook his head. "We're not going to stay long, and yes, this is the woman Brendan's been talking about."

With a nod from his father, Brendan disappeared into his room to drop his bag on his bed.

"This is a first," Steph remarked.

"Yeah," Brodie agreed slowly. He opened his mouth to elaborate, but Brendan called him. "Be right back. Try to keep the conversation to a PG rating, all right?"

"You know me. I can't make any promises," Stephanie called after him.

"Great. I'm doomed. Celeste, ignore whatever she says. It's all lies."

"Even if I said you were a god in the sack? Would that be a lie?"

He poked his head out his son's bedroom door. "Coming from you? Absolutely."

"If you're going to be like that, you were a terrible lover. Complete rubbish in bed."

Chuckling, he vanished into Brendan's room, and Stephanie turned her jade eyes on Celeste. The humor that had tinted her voice and expression half a moment before evaporated. Uncomfortable beneath the woman's intense gaze, Celeste looked away, out the front windows at the glittering lights of Butte. After the dark of the Northstar Valley, the unnatural orange glow of the rows and rows of streetlights studded by stoplights and the bluer parking lot lights of the big shopping areas was strange to her eyes.

"Please don't be uncomfortable," Stephanie remarked, drawing Celeste's attention back. "It's a compliment to you that Brodie's let you into his son's life. He's very picky about the women he even *introduces* Brendan to, and it sounds like he's done a lot more than introduce you two."

His son. Not *my* son or even *our* son, Celeste noted. "I *do* take it as a compliment, and I'm not trying to be rude. It's just a bit odd meeting you. I feel like I'm trying to take your place in their life, and I don't ever want to do that."

"Oh, honey, don't worry about that. I never claimed that place, and it was only by accident that it was even offered to me. I love Brendan, and I'm glad Brodie talked me into having him, but I'm happy with the way things are. I was never going to be the wife and mother in the fairytale family Brodie wants for Brendan. You know the kind. A mom, a dad, a couple kids, and pets, all snuggled up in a cozy house with a white picket fence or—in Brodie's case—

a cabin on the side of the ski hill with a spectacular view of the mountains he loves so much."

That sounded pretty good to Celeste, but it wasn't the picture Stephanie painted that stunned her. Only by pinching her lips between her teeth was Celeste able to contain her shock at how candidly the woman talked about her relationship with Brodie and her lack of interest in the position she'd been put in with Brendan's unplanned arrival.

"To be honest, if it had to happen, I'm glad it was with Brodie. I hate to think what would've happened to Brendan if he'd been stuck with me. Of course, if Brodie hadn't talked me out of terminating the pregnancy, I wouldn't have ever found out."

Celeste's eyes sprang wide. "You wanted an abortion?"

"I'm sorry if that offends you, but I am who I am, and I've always believed it the woman's right to decide what happens in her own body."

"No, it...." Celeste perched on the arm of the loveseat perpendicular to the couch and folded her hands in her lap. She stared at them for a long time before she answered. "That whole debate used to be a lot clearer to me, but I don't know what I believe anymore."

"There's a tragic story behind that, I'm sure, but we'll save that for some time down the road. Obviously, I didn't go through with it."

"Do you mind if I ask what changed your mind?"

"Brodie." Stephanie glanced over her shoulder down the hall. "He wanted Brendan from the moment he found out I was pregnant, and he promised I could walk away after and never look back if that's what I wanted. It challenged what I believed, and on some level, I hoped that how I felt would change, too, and that those instincts most women seem to have would magically kick in, but they didn't. I enjoy spending time with Brendan on the weekends, and I certainly don't regret having him, but I'm just not mom material. And I'm okay with that." Brendan's mother offered a polite, sympathetic smile. "Too much information?"

"No… I just can't believe how *honest* you are about it."

"Well, I see enough between you and Brodie that I think it's only fair to let you know where he and I stand." Her smile widened mischievously. "Don't want you second-guessing your relationship with him because of me."

"Do I want to know what you two are talking about in here?" Brodie inquired striding down the hall from Brendan's room with his son in tow.

"Probably not," Stephanie remarked. "It wasn't something for innocent ears… or Brendan's, either."

"Hardy har har. We forgot to pack his toothbrush, so you'll have to grab him a new one."

"I have a spare," Stephanie replied. She winked at Celeste. "I guess I'm not *totally* inept."

"You're not inept at all, and I wish you'd stop saying things like that," Brodie muttered. "Anyhow, we'd best head back. Rumor has it Russ has special plans in the works for you and Brendan tonight."

"So he said." Stephanie narrowed her eyes and pursed her lips.

Celeste glanced between the former lovers. It was clear Stephanie wanted to ask about Russ's plans, but the twinkle in Brodie's eyes said just as clearly that he wasn't going to tell. An entire conversation passed between them in an instant, and if Brodie's ex hadn't *just* explained in unsettling candor that there was nothing left between her and him but a beautiful, bright-eyed boy, Celeste might have turned tail and run. They had a history, and a long one. But it was just that—history. Without a trace of regret or anything else that might suggest Brodie's feelings for Stephanie were anything but platonic, he stooped with arms open to his son.

Brendan launched into his arms, lingering tellingly for a moment before turning to Celeste to hug her tightly. "I'm gonna miss you," he whispered.

"Aw," she murmured, giving him a good squeeze. "I'm gonna miss you, too, little man."

"See you Sunday, lad," Brodie said, ushering Celeste toward the door after Brendan finally released her. "Later, Steph."

Brodie paused on the porch out of sight of the front windows, and any lingering doubts Celeste had about where she stood with him fled when he claimed her mouth. His kiss was as passionate as his exchanges with Stephanie had been friendly, and the contrast left her breathless. He leaned away slowly, caressing her cheek with his thumb, his fingers still curled around her neck.

Her eyes widened. This was territory she'd never been in before. In the soft glow of the Christmas lights lining the porch roof, his face was beautiful in its endearing gentleness, and a promise of the love she'd only *thought* she'd found with Marc gazed back at her.

"You are something wonderful, lass," he murmured

and touched his lips to hers again—fleetingly, like the stroke of a feather—and when he drew back, she followed, rocking forward on her toes until she was fully supported against him. "I thought I knew that the moment I met you, but I'm beginning to see how shallow that first impression was."

He didn't let her respond, taking her hand and pulling her down the steps to his truck. With a sudden and childlike glee that made her head spin after their quiet moment, he hopped in behind the wheel. "Let's head home and go skinny dipping at the hot springs."

"Are you serious?"

"Of course not. The Conners would kick us out, but I *do* want to go soak. It'll help alleviate some of the tension of leaving my son with his mother."

"You're going to give me whiplash with the mood changes, Brodie. You say that like you don't trust her."

"I do, but I suffer from separation anxiety. I don't like to be away from my son."

"That's completely understandable and admirable, even. I feel like I've barely begun to get to know him," Celeste said slowly, "but I miss him already. So, yes, let's go swimming at the Ramshorn."

"And if all that bare skin and water takes us to the bedroom after…?"

The mischief in his eyes negated the intent of his words, and once again, she found herself wondering if he was intentionally steering her toward lighter-hearted conversation again. For once, she wasn't in danger of slipping into darkness, but she went with it and laughed. "I do believe that's the first time you've propositioned me. Dammit, Brodie. We had a good rhythm going, and you just threw it off. Now what do I have left to dangle in front of you?"

"Technically, I think it's the second. The first was the night we skied over to my parents' after I scared the crap out of you. And you have a *lot* left to dangle in front of me—things that will ensnare me a helluva lot tighter and longer than sex. I've had sex-based relationships before. I don't know what this is yet, but I'm damned sure it isn't that."

"Obviously not because sex is the primary component of sex-based relationships, and you keep turning me down."

"That's because you've thrown it at me like a shield rather than an invitation. Anyhow, as I said before, I knew right off that you were special, and I don't want to waste that with a shallow affair. This isn't shallow. It's… more."

"More what?"

"More everything."

"And this is a good thing?"

"This is a great thing. I thought I'd made that clear already."

"Maybe I'm just thick-skulled and need to have it spelled out in small words."

"Or maybe you're just skittish and need to be reassured."

She laughed softly. "Okay, you win."

He stopped at a red light and leaned across the cab of his truck to press a quick kiss to her lips. "Mmm. I like winning."

Their teasing conversation dwindled as he pulled onto the Interstate and had to shift his attention to the stream of holiday traffic and icy roads. Celeste let her gaze wander out the window, though there wasn't much to see once they left the glow of Butte behind—just a scattering of yard lights. Tattered clouds from the day's flurries scudded across the sky, but occasionally the stars appeared through openings in the cottony ceiling, and each time she saw them, she smiled. Would they now always make her think of Brodie?

In the silence, the implications of her conversation with Stephanie curled around her, and like a silent fog, doubt infiltrated her contentment. Brodie had talked her out of an abortion. Did that mean he believed, like so many in the bitter debate, that abortion was wrong and murder? Or had he simply been that inclined toward fatherhood? Stephanie's comments gave her hope that it was the latter, but the way the woman had described Brodie in an entirely positive light like she was trying to convince Celeste of his worth inspired more questions than it answered. Why?

"You didn't tell me Stephanie wanted an abortion," she said quietly, uncertain if she was ready for this conversation.

"She told you?"

Celeste nodded.

"What else did she say?"

"More or less that she never wanted to be a mother but she went through it for you."

"*Went through it* is about right. There were some days that I felt so guilty."

"What do you mean?"

"Pregnancy was miserable for her. First it was the acute morning sickness and then we had several close calls with preterm labor. By some miracle, Brendan was born only two weeks early, and Stephanie was so certain she never wanted to go through it all again that she had a tubal ligation on the spot."

"She didn't consider that you might want more kids?"

"I'm the one who suggested it. By that point, I think we were both pretty sure it wouldn't last, and even if we *had* managed to make it work, I don't think I could've watched her go through that again. I might not have ever been *in* love with her, but I did and still do care deeply for her, and I've never been able to stand seeing anyone I love in pain. Besides," he added, giving Celeste's hand a squeeze. "Her body, her choice. And for her to go through that so I could have my son.… I'm a damned lucky guy."

"You're a fool for feeling guilty, Brodie," Celeste murmured. "She's lucky to have had you to give her the security and support through it all. And I believe she'd tell you the same."

He glanced at her, frowning for a moment. Then he smiled. "I know she'd tell me the same because she has. Doesn't change how I feel, though."

"You wouldn't be you if it did."

Needing to be close to him, she unbuckled her seatbelt and scooted into the narrow center seat, strapped herself in, and rested her head on his shoulder. She teetered on the edge of spilling all her dark secrets, but the way her hands trembled told her she wasn't quite ready. She wasn't sure enough of herself or their relationship yet, and while his comments reassured her, she wasn't brave enough to ask for the solid confirmation that he wouldn't turn from her in disgust when he learned what she'd done. For the moment, she clung to him with tears burning her eyes, closer than she'd ever been to fully giving in to the grief… and closer to stepping fully out of the numbness to embrace it and, after, to let it go.

How differently things might've turned out if Marc had been more like Brodie and I hadn't been terrified to tether myself to him with a child.

Eight

SOMETHING HAD CHANGED in the eight days since Celeste's talk with Stephanie, and Brodie wondered what his ex had said to her in those short few minutes they'd had alone. Whatever it was, it had made a distinct impression. He hadn't seen a trace of her reckless anger in the time since, and at the moment, she was currently singing along with the Christmas song emanating from the ski lodge's stereo system—the song Shannon had written the day Ty had proposed, *Mistletoe Kisses*—as she perched precariously atop the ladder to tack the glittery tinsel garland around the windows. Even if the view out those windows weren't hidden in darkness, it would've had a hard time competing with Celeste's beauty.

It wasn't the air of joviality about her; he'd seen plenty of that the night he and Brendan and Shannon and

Ty had helped decorate her cabin and caught brief glimpses even before that. What exactly *it* was, he couldn't quite pin down, but the word *relaxed* came to mind. Or maybe *open*. Rather than enclosing herself within walls of tense defensiveness and heartache, she was almost effervescent.

"You gonna finish those reports, or what?" Ainsley asked, setting a steaming cup of coffee on the table beside him. "I thought you were supposed to have dinner with Celeste after work."

"I am." He sat back and rolled his neck and shoulders to ease some of the ache from sitting hunched over his paperwork for too long out of them, lifted the mug toward his sister in a show of gratitude, and took a sip.

She snorted. "When? Midnight?"

"Keep it up, sprite," he muttered, "and I'll take your Christmas present back to the store and find the nastiest congealed cow turd in the pasture to put in your stocking."

"You'd never do that. You love me too much."

"Doesn't mean I can't pay you back for being a pain in my arse."

Ainsley draped herself around his shoulders and whispered, "I'd ask if you two had done the deed, but her bliss seems a little one-sided, so I'm thinking not."

"Not that it's any of your business, but no, we haven't."

"I'm surprised, considering her total lack of subtlety about her interest in you from the get-go."

"You know this isn't helping me get my work done, right? And since I *would* in fact like to have a few hours to spend with Celeste this evening, flutter off, sprite."

She kissed his cheek and zipped around the counter,

vanishing into the kitchen to finish cleaning it for the night. Brodie returned his attention to his end-of-day bookkeeping with a renewed zeal, all the more eager to get out of here after his sister's comments. During the day, with the lodge packed with weekend skiers and snowboarders, it hadn't been too difficult to keep his hands off Celeste, but now that they were mostly alone in the lodge, all he wanted was to gather her in his arms, absorb that light, and wrap her soul around him. He didn't know if it was possible to immerse himself in another's spirit, but that's exactly what he wanted to do.

Slender hands slid over his shoulders and across his chest, and the way every cell in his body sang at her touch, he knew it wasn't his sister.

"I'm all done, boss."

"I'm not."

"So I see. Do you want me to stick around or should I head home and get dinner started so it's ready when you get there?"

"Of course I want you to stick around," he quipped, "but that's exactly why I need you to go. I don't know what all Stephanie said to you last Friday, but ever since, you've had this luminescence about you, and it's damned distracting."

"I do, do I?"

"Mmm-hmm. What did she say to you?"

"I already told you what she said."

"She had to have said something else."

"It's more how what she said opened my eyes."

"About what?"

"About you and us. About me. There are a lot of

things I've been hard on myself about, and while I can't say I've forgiven myself for them yet, I have enough perspective now to see that maybe I can. That maybe I *should*." She tightened her arms around him and sighed. "We can't have a real chance if I don't. And I want us to have that chance even though I'm still terrified I'll keep making the same mistakes my mother makes and that I made with Marc."

What the hell had that prick done to her? "You say you want us to have a chance, but you aren't telling me why."

"Because I trust you. And I trust that you're different."

Curiosity needled him, but the radiance had dimmed, so he ignored it and instead craned his head around to kiss her, careful to keep a tight grip on his desire.

"You amaze me, lass," he whispered. "See you at home in a bit. We'll talk more then."

After she left, it was considerably easier to focus on his job, and by the time Ainsley finished the kitchen, he was ready to lock up. He dropped her off at her cabin at the base of Lightning Ridge Road and stopped only for a moment at his place to check on his animals before he headed up to Celeste's A-frame. In contrast to how dark the structure's windows had been that first night he'd met her, tonight they glowed brightly in the inky night with the lights of her Christmas tree twinkling amongst the branches as he drove up the hill.

He let himself into the mudroom, and as soon as the door swung open, a mouthwatering aroma greeted him. She'd made something Italian, and if it tasted anything like it smelled, he was in for a treat. His stomach growled, reminding him that he hadn't eaten lunch today. Hurriedly, he kicked off his boots and shrugged out of his coat. Remembering her tendency to startle easily, he knocked hard enough to make his knuckles complain and hoped she could hear it over her music—Shannon's second album this evening, Brodie's favorite of the two Celeste's friend had so far released because it showcased her powerhouse voice better than her comparatively cautious debut album did. The song blaring from the speakers of Celeste's computer was the one with a hint of discord and kiss-my-ass confidence. Hopefully that didn't mean Celeste's mood had further darkened since she'd left the ski hill.

When his knock received no answer, he knocked again. Still nothing. He cautiously opened the door to find dinner simmering on the stove and Bard sprawled in front of the wood stove as usual. When he spotted Brodie in the kitchen, the big cat yawned and meowed in greeting but made no move to leave the warmth of the fire.

Lazy fur ball, Brodie mused fondly.

Celeste was ensconced in her work area in the right corner of the living room, facing the windows with her back to Brodie and entirely immersed in her work. Watercolor he guessed as she dipped her brush repeatedly in glass of the water beside her. The tilt of the contraption she'd set on the table wasn't high enough for him to see what she was painting, but there was a lot of rich spring green interspersed with flashes of sienna.

"I'm here at last," he called.

She jumped, clipping her water glass with her elbow, but with lightning reflexes, she caught it before it tumbled off the table. Only a few drops sloshed over the rim to splatter on the table's scarred top. She swiveled in her chair to face Brodie with her hand over her heart. Then, to his delight, she shook her head and smiled.

"You really have to stop scaring the crap out of me," she said breathlessly, "or I'm going to have a heart attack before I hit thirty."

"Hey, this time it isn't my fault. You knew I was coming. Whatcha working on, lass?"

"Come see."

He strode across the house to inspect her painting. When he reached her, Bard finally decided it was worth the effort to get up to greet him properly, so he bent down to pick the cat up while he perused the painting. It appeared to be finished, or nearly so, and was a breathtakingly detailed scene. Redwoods towered over a pond, and there were ripples on the water's otherwise glassy surface from drops falling from the gargantuan trees' branches. Leaning closer, he noticed the shape of a young girl sitting against the base of one of the trees with her knees drawn up to her chest and her face buried against them. Suddenly, the strikingly beautiful image turned achingly sad. The girl wasn't quite finished yet, but the long dark hair cascading about her shoulders reminded him forcefully of Celeste's in the photo of her and Shannon at the ski hill last year.

"Is this for a client?" he wondered aloud, recalling that she'd said she hadn't felt much like painting for herself recently.

"No," she replied, sounding a little surprised at herself. "It's for me. First one I've been able to do since…."

"Tell me about it," he invited when almost a minute passed and she hadn't spoken again. "How did you come up with the redwoods?"

"I was born in Santa Rosa, California, and we lived in a little cottage in the redwoods near Guerneville. I remember it being dark all the time, always in the shade of those amazing trees, but every time I've tried to paint them… they always come out bright, like this, and now I wonder if that's because the only peace I knew in that house was by that pond." She tilted her head, studying the image with narrowed eyes. "It wasn't even a pond. It was a giant puddle that showed up every time it rained, but it was so beautiful, the way the drops glittered as they fell, especially after the rain when the sun came out. It was magical."

"I can see that." He hesitated a moment. Was she distracted enough by the memory of that magic to allow him to probe deeper? *Gently*, he decided. *Proceed gently.* "Why was that pond the only place where you found peace?"

"My parents were always fighting. Screaming at each other. Breaking things. Until my father had enough, and then he'd hit Mom to get her to shut up. And she let him. When they started fighting, I'd run out and hide by the pond and wait for it to be over. Rain or shine, it didn't matter. That was my safe place, where I could pretend that darkness didn't exist."

Brodie swore under his breath. The women in her family didn't have much luck with men? That was putting it mildly. "Did he ever hit you?"

"No. Just my mother, but I was only seven when we left, and it's possible I would've eventually become a target, too."

"What made her finally leave?"

"This." Celeste rolled the right leg of her soft blue

jeans up to reveal a thick white scar on her knee. "He was drunk one night, and he started in on my mother about who knows what, and I'd had enough, so when he charged her after she threw a glass at him, I tried to stop him, and he knocked me out of the way. I fell on the broken glass, and it took eight stitches to close this up. I guess my mother was okay with being his punching bag, but when I got hurt trying to protect her, it was too much."

Brodie didn't like the chill that crept into her voice. "Have you seen or talked to him since?"

She shook her head. "We moved to Silverdale— about twenty miles from where Shannon and I lived—and moved in with my Grandma Letty."

"Your mom's mom?"

"No, Gran Sylvia died when Mom was only thirteen, but her husband was exactly the same, and Mom denies it, but I know Gran died because she couldn't take any more. There was nothing medically wrong with her." She sighed. "Letty is my father's mother. Her husband was abusive, too, so she divorced him and moved to Silverdale, and when my father started turning out to be exactly like *his* father, she disowned him. She tried to warn my mother, but Mom isn't strong like Grandma Letty. She was, is, and probably always will be a starry-eyed dreamer who thinks there's good in even the darkest hearts. I suppose she doesn't know any better."

"A vicious cycle," he murmured. "And what about you? Do you know better?"

"That's what terrifies me, Brodie. I was still pretty young when my parents divorced, but...."

All the pieces he'd been gathering for weeks now fell

into place, and the picture that appeared was not a pleasant one. Abruptly, he set Bard on the floor and straightened. He didn't need clarification right now, didn't need to hear her say she thought he could ever be like the men who had taught her only fear. He needed to chase the shadows away before the shuddering flicker of light blew out again. "All right, that's enough talk about the past for one night."

In that one-shouldered halter top that reminded him strongly of the bathing suit she'd worn the night they'd met, she was entirely sexy and should have evoked a raging desire to take her upstairs to her bed in the loft, but the vulnerability in her wide eyes was once again too reminiscent of a frightened doe. When her lip quivered and tears brimmed in those pleading eyes, it nearly fractured him.

"No, no, no, lass," he whispered. "Don't let the shadows bury your light again. Please. Come back to me, Celeste."

The first tear slipped silently down her cheek. "You don't want to be with me, Brodie."

"Yes, I do."

She shook her head. "No, you don't. You think you, do but you don't. I'm broken."

He wasn't going to try to convince her she wasn't, because it was the truth that she was, but that didn't mean she couldn't repair herself. Look at how many pieces she'd already put back together! "Don't do that, Celeste. Only I get to decide if I want to be with you, and I swear to you that I do. I've never been in the habit of throwing a soul away just because it's been damaged, and I'm damned sure not going to start now."

Prove it. The thought came to him with a frantic intensity, followed immediately by despair. *How? What can I possibly say to make her believe me?*

Seconds ticked by, each one faster than the last, and he felt her closing him out. *Words aren't enough. Show her.*

He clasped her face and kissed her, tenderly at first but he escalated it until the length of her body was crushed to his. He poured everything into that kiss, and the fierceness of it shocked him, as if this was his one chance to secure the future he'd started building around her. After a moment's hesitation, she responded in kind. Rather than cooling the fervor, her engagement propelled it to new heights. The salt of her tears melded with the sweet taste of her, and he broke the kiss long enough to slide an arm behind her shoulders and knees and lifted her off the ground. He turned his head to kiss her again as he carried her to the couch—damn, she was so tiny—but she was already there, and when she threaded her fingers through his hair, he groaned.

He sat on the couch with her in his lap. He wanted to lay her down and skim his hands over her body, but if he did that, there was no way he'd be able to stop, and now was not the time to lose control. Rather than continue on the path their bodies obviously wanted to rocket down, he cradled her against his chest, stroking his hand over her silky hair and bare shoulders.

She wasn't wearing any black or gray today, he realized suddenly. While her top reminded him of her swimsuit, it wasn't black but burgundy and navy. Dark colors, yes, but *color*. He held her closer and tried to swallow the lump in his throat.

"You believe I want to be with you now?" he asked hoarsely.

She nodded, chewing on her lip. He wiped the tears from her cheeks with his thumbs and kissed the top of her head.

"Good. Why don't you sit here while I dish us up some of that delicious dinner you made? Anything special I need to do with it?"

"No, but I can do—"

"Stay here," he said quietly but firmly. "Give yourself a moment, okay? I'll get dinner."

That she let him help was another victory. It showed him that she could set aside her innate need to be independent and accept that letting him do this for her didn't mean she was weak. He caught sight of her notecard on the doorframe as he set the table.

"I think you need a new motivational notecard to put here," he remarked when she joined him in the kitchen. "Because you're already saving yourself."

"Am I?"

"Absolutely."

"What do you suggest I put in its place?"

He set the stack of plates on the table and drew her against him again. Brushing his fingertips along her jaw and cheek before combing her hair back from her face, he dipped his head to kiss her. She yielded with the same brilliance that had dazzled him all day, and still holding her face in his hands, he whispered, "The stars shine brightest in the darkest nights."

* * *

"Brodie, Brendan, I don't know what you're doing to

her," Shannon remarked, twisting her poker slowly over the fire as the marshmallow skewered on the end turned a perfect golden brown, "but it's working. This is the first time she's held Jack."

Her friend said it quietly enough that Celeste didn't think she was supposed to have heard it, so she gave no sign that she had, instead choosing to focus her attention on the three-month-old baby in her arms while she eavesdropped.

"I'm pretty sure we had very little to do with it," Brodie replied so softly she almost couldn't hear him. Further proof that theirs wasn't a conversation she was meant to hear... which only made it that much more irresistible. "She's just that strong. Nothing you or I or anyone else could do would've brought her to this point so fast if she wasn't."

Celeste tried to hold back the smile, but it slipped her grasp, lifting her lips with shy gratitude. She couldn't say how far she'd come, and perhaps she was too close to see it, but if she had, she disagreed with Brodie. Without him and his charming son and their willingness to put up with her volatile moods with unshakeable patience, who or what would've shown her that it was okay to feel like the ground was falling out from under her while she found her feet?

As heat clawed up her neck and across her face, she tilted her face down so the only person who could see it was the only one too young to notice. Jack held her gaze, as mesmerized by her eyes as she was by his, and it seemed silly now that she had been so terrified of him. That didn't stop her from trembling with a surge of conflicting emotions, most of which had no place in her heart tonight, but she *was* in a place that she could allow herself this weakness. With the laughter of her friends—Shannon, Ty, Brodie, his son and his parents and sister—warming the still winter night air, the pure silver light of a waxing gibbous moon coaxing blue sparkles from the snow, and the radiant heat of the popping fire in the pit in the front yard of her A-frame, she should be utterly at peace with the world and everything in it. Perhaps she was. When Shannon had asked her for the thousandth time since she'd come to Northstar if she wanted to hold Jack, she hadn't said no, and in fact, she'd hesitated only a second before saying yes.

And he was such a beautiful little boy, she thought, tugging his blankets a little tighter around him to ward off the night's chill. To be fair, it wasn't *him* she'd been afraid of; it was what he reminded her of. A sly, destructive voice whispered in the back of her mind. *You could've had this.*

No. Stubbornly, she refused to give into it. Jack was the product of love and respect and a million other things she'd never had with Marc. *I wouldn't have had this. I would've had a noose.*

"Well, folks, it's been fun," Shannon announced, stepping over to Celeste, "but it's time for us to call it a night. This was a good idea, Celeste. Thank you."

Celeste nodded in acknowledgement and stood to hand Jack back to his mother, at once reluctant and relieved. "I'm sorry I picked a night when everyone had to get up early, but I wanted Brendan to be able to join us."

The boy hugged her around her waist, and she hugged him back. After Ty and Shannon left, the rest of her guests returned to their benches, and they sat in companionable silence, enjoying the moon and stars, the fire, and the simplicity of each other's company. Brendan stayed beside Celeste, snuggled up to her side, and she didn't realize it until she happened to glance at Brodie. He watched them with an odd smile. There was an emotion in his eyes she couldn't name, but his approval of his son's attachment to her and of hers to his son was plainly evident in the curve of his lips. She noted the glances between him and his parents and sister, and though not one of them said a word, she could guess at their unspoken conversation.

They cared about her, and more, they approved of Brodie's relationship with her. Perhaps more than they'd approved of his other relationships.

Again, her face warmed but this time with gratitude and pride rather than embarrassment.

Angus stood and held his hand out to his wife. "Time for us to turn in, too," he said. He embraced Celeste and Brendan together. "Thanks for invitin' us, lass."

"It was my pleasure, Angus. It's the least I can do to thank you for all you and your family have done for me."

"Ah, Celeste, love, you've brought us—and I believe, will continue to bring us—much joy."

"Thank you."

Sula embraced her next. "God's honest truth. You've brought some of the light back into this family that we lost when Inez died."

Celeste jerked back, gaping. "How can that be when I feel like I'm caught in the shadows?"

The older woman gave her shoulder a squeeze. "When you figure that out for yourself, you won't have to ask. And I suspect that about that time, we'll all be hearing bells."

"Bells?"

Sula didn't answer. She only smiled, took her husband's hand, and walked with him to the back of the house where they'd left their skis. A few minutes later, Celeste glanced over her shoulder and saw them gliding toward home on the trail Brodie had taken her on that night a couple weeks ago. She turned back to the fire only to find Ainsley standing in front of her, waiting to hug her goodnight. In short order, Brodie's sprite of a sister was gone, too, and almost before she was ready, Brodie was beside her, announcing it was time for him to take Brendan home to put him to bed.

"As you seem to be in more of a contemplative than celebratory mood, I don't think you'll miss us too much," he remarked.

"Oh, don't be too sure about that. I already miss you both."

"How can you miss us when we're right here?" Brendan asked.

She gave him a squeeze. "I miss you because you'll be gone in a minute, and my heart is already saying goodbye. Like when you miss your dad on Friday when he drops you off at your mom's. You know you won't see him for a couple days, so you start to miss him even before he's gone, right?"

"Yeah… I never thought of it like that."

"Come on, Brendan," Brodie said. "It's too late to play twenty questions. Save it for tomorrow after school. Maybe Celeste will be nice and let you play it all the way down the ski hill."

"You're gonna let me snowboard the whole hill? With Celeste?"

"If she's willing to put up with you for that long." Brodie looked questioningly at her.

"I'd love to."

"Good. That means I might actually get ahead on my backlog of skis and boards to wax."

"You won't be coming with us?"

"I hadn't planned on it."

Celeste held his gaze for almost a minute, probing his sincerity. In their time together, he had given her a pretty firm impression that he didn't trust too many people with his son, and she was deeply touched that he apparently trusted her enough to take Brendan down the slopes— something that had the potential to be dangerous. Impulsively, she rocked to her feet and threw her arms around Brodie's neck.

"Thank you," she whispered.

"Don't know why you're thanking me for foisting my kid off on you for an hour or two."

His words were joking, as they often were, but once again, his tone took away some of the lightheartedness and replaced it with warmth.

"Thank you for trusting me with your son. It means a lot to me. In your place, I'm not sure I'd be so understanding."

"That's because you can't see what I see."

His kiss—with his son looking on—said more than words could, and she melted into him. Too soon, he relinquished her mouth, and she prepared herself to say good night to him and Brendan. He didn't immediately let her go, instead leaning back with his hands knitted behind her back, and his gaze as he studied her was intense enough to make her squirm… but she didn't.

"May I ask you a question, lass?" he inquired, his voice barely more than a whisper.

"Sure."

"Aside from the couple times I scared the hell out of you, have I ever given you a reason to feel anything less than safe with me?"

Celeste jerked back. The question came out of nowhere, and was so far from the endearing good night she'd expected that she could only stare at him with her mouth agape for several thudding beats of her heart. "N-no," she stammered at last.

"Good."

"Why… what made you ask that?"

"Something you said about your chat with Steph has been chewing on me. Don't worry about it." He dipped his head to kiss her again. "If you're headed off to bed after we leave, may the stars guard you dreams. If you're planning to while away half the night in whatever artistic endeavor your heart desires, happy creating. Good night, lass."

Brendan stood on the bench he and Celeste had so recently vacated and wrapped his arms tightly around her. "See you at the ski hill tomorrow?"

"You bet. I can't wait."

After they left, Celeste enjoyed the quiet crinkling of the dying fire for a few minutes before she doused it and headed inside. Bard, in his usual spot beside the wood stove, meowed plaintively, so she picked him up and carried him to her desk chair, then settled him on her lap. She woke her iMac and stared at its screen for a moment, tapping her fingers on the mouse. It wasn't late enough to even think about preparing for bed—the clock in the upper right of her screen read 8:27 PM—and even if it were, a curious energy pulsed through her, at once inciting a need to work on *something* and scattering her focus so she couldn't decide what. She could finish that cover she'd started this morning, or she could finish her redwood painting, or she could start something new. Her fingers twitched, and suddenly, she thought it might be fun to sketch. But what?

And what was with that question of Brodie's? What had she said about her talk with Stephanie? And what had he read into it? She'd answered him honestly, at least, in her shock. She *did* feel safe with him even though her experiences with Marc should have made that impossible.

Sighing, she turned her gaze toward the kitchen and noticed a flashing light on her answering machine.

"Oh, crap," she said, rising to her feet again and settling Bard on her chair. "Grandma Letty was supposed to call tonight."

Sure enough, the single message on the machine was from her grandmother, and the sound of the woman's strong, cherished voice brought a smile to Celeste's face and quelled the restless indecision. The message was a simple, "Sorry I missed you. I'll call you tomorrow."

Celeste didn't feel like waiting until tomorrow to talk to her grandmother, so she snatched the cordless from its base and dialed Letty's number.

"You didn't have to call me back tonight, dear," the older woman greeted. "I hope you didn't cut whatever fun you were having short because of me."

"No. I forgot you said you were going to call. Sorry, Grandma."

"So long as you *were* having fun, there's no need to apologize."

"I was. I invited Shannon and Ty and Brodie and his family up for a fire, s'mores, and hot chocolate."

"Sounds delightful. And you sound happy, which makes me think things are going well with your gentleman friend. How is Brodie?"

"He's… great, but I can't help thinking I'm missing something."

"You're a smart woman, Celeste, and you're wiser now than you were when you met Marc."

"Maybe, but what if I'm doomed to the same cycle of choosing bad men Mom is?"

"Brodie doesn't sound like a bad man. From what you've told me—most especially the parts about his son— make me believe he's a very good man."

"And you've heard it all through me, so your impression is viewed through the biased and possibly faulty lens of *my* impression."

"My sweet girl, you are not your mother. You are stronger than she is."

"How do you figure? I fell into the exact same trap she did."

"And the same one I fell into when I married your grandfather. But I fought it and won, and so did you. Maybe I never married again, but I didn't fall into the trap a second time, either, and neither will you. You've seen evil now, Celeste. You know all about its smooth charms and what they hide, and your sense of self worth won't let you make that mistake again because you know you deserve better."

"Then how do you explain Marc?"

"You have had precious little experience with men, sweet girl, and a girl almost always goes for one like her daddy the first time because it's what she knows. You met Marc right out of college, and he was a charming bastard—I'll give him that. He even had *me* charmed for a while. Before him, how many boys did you date?"

"Two."

"Two," Letty repeated. "And neither of them were ever contenders. You were shy and wary of boys, and most of the boys were just as shy and wary of you. But Marc wasn't. And if you hadn't known him through Lane, if he'd met you first at the corner coffee shop and asked you out as a stranger, I doubt you ever would've said yes to him. But you grew to know him over a period of years, and so you innocently believed you were as safe with him as you were with Lane because he was a friend, too."

Safe. There's that word again.

The way Letty painted it, it should be easy to forgive herself for her error in judgment, but Celeste winced at the mention of her friend. She and Lane had been the best of friends in high school and even in college despite attending schools at opposite ends of the state, and Celeste's return to Kingston and later her marriage to Lane's brother had reinvigorated their friendship. Marc's death and the chain of events leading up to it had done what distance had not and closed the door on them. When last she'd spoken to Lane after the chaos of his death had quieted some, they had addressed one another like polite strangers or uncomfortable business partners, which they had been until all the paperwork had been signed for Lane to take over Marc's business. Now they weren't even that.

She slid onto one of the stools at the kitchen's island and, resting her elbow on the counter, dropped her chin into her hand with her palm over her mouth and her fingers drumming against her cheek. She inhaled, held it, and let the breath out slowly.

"That's all well and good, but that doesn't mean I won't make the same mistake again. I still have about as much experience with men as I did before I married Marc."

"Find a happily married woman who is treated by her husband the way you would want to be treated by yours… and take a good long look at him. You're an artist. Use that eye of yours to see beyond the obvious."

The first man that came to mind was Ty, and while she knew he was nothing like Marc, she hadn't known him long enough to get as clear a picture of how and why as she wanted. The second man she thought of was Shannon's brother, Pat. She closed her eyes and let her mind revisit all her encounters with him. He and Aelissm had been married for twelve years now, and Celeste recalled watching them dance together in the Bedspread last Christmas with a tickle of envy. She ignored the overt gestures—the kisses, the hugs, the open laughter; Marc had been plenty skilled at those. Instead, she paid close attention to the more subtle details like those faint, poignant smiles when Pat's gaze found its way to Aeli when she wasn't looking, the way he leaned toward her when she spoke, and how he couldn't seem to resist sliding his fingers across her back as she walked past. She thought, too, of how Ty had been willing to give up everything he'd built with his horse training business to support Shannon's dreams and of how he looked at his wife much the same way as Pat looked at

Aelissm.

"Ty and Pat look at Shannon and Aelissm like plants tilted toward the sun. Like Shannon and Aeli are the light they need to thrive."

"And did Marc ever look at you like that?"

"No." The answer was quick and decisive, and even after she'd had a moment to analyze it, she knew it was right.

"The next time you and Brodie are together, why don't you see if he looks at you how you say Ty and Pat look at their wives? In the meantime, call your mother."

For the second time tonight, an abrupt comment left her temporarily speechless. "I just emailed her yesterday."

"I know that, but she's called me three times today to say you haven't responded to the emails she's sent."

Celeste strode back to her desk and, leaning over her cat-occupied chair, logged in to her email. Sure enough, there were a dozen emails from her mother, and in true Dawn fashion, not one of the them said anything to give her a clue about whatever urgent topic was on her mother's mind. Celeste let her head fall. She was in a good mood, and a talk with her mother was likely to sour it. "Did she tell you what she wants?"

"Of course not."

With a sigh, Celeste promised to call Dawn.

"All right, dear. It's your turn to call me next. Talk to you in a couple days?"

"Mmm-hmm. Love you, Grandma."

"Love you, too, sweet girl."

Celeste ended the call and set her cordless on her desk, then stared at it for several minutes. She was tempted to just email her mother back and ask what was so urgent that she'd sent a dozen emails but not so urgent that she hadn't just picked up the phone and called, but then she'd end up sitting around waiting for her mother to reply as annoyance and tension steadily built and ruined whatever chance she had of getting any work done tonight. Finally, she plucked the phone off her desk and started to dial her mother's number only to realize she couldn't remember it. What a sad state of affairs that she called her mother so rarely anymore that she couldn't remember her California number. With a growl, she looked the number up in the contacts on her iMac, dialed it, and wandered over to the big windows as it rang.

"Hello?" Dawn answered after the seventh ring.

"It's Celeste. Grandma said you're trying—"

"Where have you been?" her mother demanded with a note of hysteria in her voice.

Celeste rolled her eyes and sighed. "I worked at the ski hill all day, and then I had some friends over for a fire. Why didn't you just call me?"

"I don't have the phone number to your cabin."

Celeste swore she'd given the number to her mother, but maybe she'd only thought to do it and hadn't actually done it. Dawn hadn't been very high up on her list of priorities since she'd moved back to California and rented a house too close to Celeste's father. Dawn denied it any time she was asked, but Celeste was fairly certain she and Phil had been in contact. Of course, Dawn had found a new man to take care of her, so for the time being, reconciliation was unlikely. Small mercies.

"You could've asked Grandma for it."

"I did. She said if you hadn't given it to me, you didn't

want me to have it."

"I thought I did. Sorry, Mom. Anyhow, I have some artwork I'd like to make some progress on tonight, so what did you need?"

"Lane called. She's been trying to track you down for a while now. She said she has some paperwork she needs you to sign."

"I signed everything. Marc's business and all his belongings are hers, free and clear."

"She said it was something you missed. Would you please call her?"

Celeste glanced at the clock again. It was now just after nine—just after eight in Washington—but it was late enough that a call to Lane could be considered rude, and at any rate, Marc's sister was the last person she wanted to talk to right now. What was left of her good mood would surely disintegrate. "It's getting late, but I promise I'll call her tomorrow. Is there anything else?"

"No, that was it." There was a pause on the other end of the line, and the only sound that interrupted the silence was the nervous tapping of her mother's fingers against the phone. "How are you? You sound tired."

"I wasn't until just a few minutes ago. I had quite a lovely evening with Shannon and Ty and Brodie and his family."

"You seem to be spending a lot of time with this Brodie fellow. Are you sure that's a good idea? I mean, it just seems too soon to move on from Marc...."

Celeste snapped straight, scowling. "You're not exactly one who should be giving advice about men, Mother, considering how many empty beer bottles, cuts, and black eyes litter your track record. Or have you already forgotten what breed of asshole my father was?”

“Celeste—”

“And this new man of yours. He’s looking to be just like him.”

“Celeste Aurora Dawson!”

“No. Brodie is a good man from a loving, supportive family. If I’d found someone like him first, I never would’ve ended up with a son of a bitch carved from the same alcoholic tree as my dear old dad. Maybe you’re happy to let men use and abuse you, but I’m not, Mother. I. Am. Not. I’d rather be alone for the rest of my life than subject myself to that.”

Silence deeper than the last greeted her assertion, and minutes ticked by with no response. Celeste’s body quivered with the force of her conviction… and with the shock that she meant and believed every word of it.

At last, quiet crying issued from the earpiece, and Celeste let out a breath in a huff that tailed off into a sigh. “I’m sorry, Mom. I don’t mean to be so harsh. Maybe we should just stick to emails.”

“No,” Dawn choked. “Please, Celeste. I feel like I’m losing my daughter, and I can’t bear it.”

Celeste sank onto the chair by the front door, hunched over her knees with her eyes fixed on the new notecard she’d tacked to the kitchen door. It was too far away to read the golden letters or to see the watercolor night sky she’d painted, but the words on it and the memory of Brodie suggesting them brought a tired smile to her face. *The stars shine brightest in the darkest nights.* “Then try being optimistic for once and happy that I’ve found a glimmer of peace and hope."

Dawn sniffed. "You're right. I should be happy for you, and I promise I'll try to be optimistic."

Celeste hoped her mother meant it, but even though Dawn was one of the most optimistic people she knew, her optimism always sprang from the worst places—like the chance that there might be an inkling of redeeming value in the jerks she dated. When it came to having faith in good things, Dawn had none, perhaps because there had been so few in her life. Celeste didn't know if refusing to confine herself to that cage was enough to break the bars and free herself, but it certainly couldn't hurt, right?

"I guess that'll have to do," she murmured.

She ended the call without making any promises about when she'd call again, still unsure if she would. She *had* found peace and hope here in Northstar, and a *lot* more than a mere glimmer of it, and if tonight's conversation with her mother was any indication, opening the door to the anguish that always accompanied her talks with Dawn would dim it.

No longer buoyed by that wonderful energy, she shut her computer down for the night and trudged upstairs to bed with her cat following behind.

Nine

IT WAS THREE DAYS before Celeste gathered the willpower to call Lane. She should have just called her Wednesday night, because the prospect of talking to her old friend had dogged her since, and by now, her neck and shoulders ached from the tension. Part of her hoped Lane wouldn't answer, and the rest just wanted to get it over and done with so she could forget about it and focus on having a fun evening with Brodie. And get to testing her grandmother's hypothesis.

"Apple Blossom Boutique and Marcus Lamb Fashion, this is Lane speaking. How may I help you?"

"Lane, it's Celeste. My mother said you needed me to sign something?"

"Oh, hi, Celeste. Yeah. I went to put together a catalogue of Marcus's last spring line, and it looks like you never signed those release forms."

"What release forms?"

"For the photographs of the clothing you modeled for Marcus."

"I signed release forms when he took them."

"The new ones. The old ones gave permission only to my brother."

"What new ones? I signed everything you gave me when you took over his business."

"Apparently you didn't. I wish you would've made sure everything was one hundred percent in order before you decided to flit off to Montana."

Flit off to Montana? "First of all, you never gave me new release forms for those photos. Secondly, I had to do something to get away from the memories of Marc before they drove me irreparably insane."

"I *did* send you those release forms, but whatever. I can send you more. And I guess I just don't understand why you left. If it were me, I'd want to hold on to the good memories of my husband."

Celeste's mouth fell open. Lane knew *exactly* what had happened that night as well as everything—*everything*—that had preceded it. "Do you really not know who your brother was? Are you so besotted with your childhood fantasy of him that you…. You know what? Never mind. Send me the damned release forms so I can be done with you and your whole goddamned family once and for all."

God, what she wouldn't give to have a phone to slam. Instead, she jabbed the call-end button and hurled the cordless handset at her couch. Anger rippled through her, but she had enough sense left to know that launching the phone at the wall across the room wasn't a good idea. After a moment, she realized she hadn't given Lane her address. There was no way in hell she was going to call the woman back right now; restless fury churned beneath the surface, desiring release, and if she so much as heard one more thing about Marc or his business, she'd lose it.

She almost longed for the numbness, but she'd gotten too used to feeling again, and even this seething anger was welcome. She *was* recovering. She *would* heal from this god-awful nightmare. The color of it, too—the burning reds and oranges—were welcome after those months of blackness. She sank onto the couch with her hands pressed between her knees as other colors cooled the flames. Brodie came to mind, and immediately, she thought of rich blue midnight spattered with pinpricks of pure white light.

I'm thinking in colors again. A waft of relief chased away the rage, and her lips curved. *I've missed this.*

An image danced into her mind—the amethyst rose she'd pictured when she'd made the decision to spend a couple months in Northstar that had been among the first hints of color in her thoughts following Marc's death—and glancing at the clock on the phone, she rose from the couch and stepped over to her work area. It was still late morning, so she had hours yet until she needed to start prepping dinner for Brodie. Plenty of time to bring that rose to life. On her tilted worktable, she arranged her watercolors and a large sheet of watercolor paper, all supplies Shannon and Ty had given her. Her lips lifted a little more.

Thank God for true friends.

She got to work, stopping occasionally to pet Bard. He perched on her desk chair to watch her work, as he usually did, and she paused for a moment to wonder what it was he found so fascinating. Perhaps it was the movements of her brush. Or maybe he really was a golden retriever trapped in a cat's body and he liked her artwork because it was a part of her soul on paper.

"You're a sweet boy, Bard," she murmured.

The rose took shape, its velvety petals decorated with glittering dewdrops. It also took on a tint closer to lavender toward the center though the tips of the petals were a deep, rich amethyst. Interesting. Did the creativity and possibility of the darker hue bleed into the love and majesty evoked by the lighter purple, or was it the other way around? Behind it, a fiery sunset in the lower portion of the paper gave way to a starry midnight at the top. If her detailed, realistic painting of the pond amidst the redwoods of her childhood was representative of memory, this was an expression of her spirit as it should be—on fire and free, gleaming in colors brighter than real life with swirls of stars that bordered on the abstract.

When every inch of the paper was drenched in color, She stood back and let her eyes wander over it, taking in the vibrant hues and graceful brush strokes, and nodded. It was done. It wasn't her most detailed painting, but that was right. The emotion in it was uncomplicated and open and would've been lost in too many details.

"What do you think, Bard?"

Her companion meowed and stretched to head-butt her hand, so she lavished him with eyebrow rubs and chin scratches. He rewarded her with his trademark rumbling purr.

She gathered her brushes and paints and started

cleaning up. Just as she was arranging her brushes on a paper towel to dry, her phone rang. The clock on the base said it was almost four in the afternoon. Maybe it was Brodie calling from the ski hill. She grabbed the cordless from the couch cushion where she'd left it and answered the call.

"Hello?"

"Are you through being a bitch?"

Lane.

Every muscle that had loosened over the last several hours immediately tightened again. She ground her teeth. "Since you asked like that, no, I'm not. Call me back when *you're* done being a bitch, and we'll talk."

She jerked the phone away from her ear and moved her thumb to the call-end button.

"Celeste, wait!"

After a moment's hesitation, she brought the phone back to her ear. She took a deep breath and raked her hair back from her face. On the exhale, she muttered, "What?"

"You forgot to give me your address so I can send these forms to you."

Right. That. She quickly rattled off the cabin's mailing address. "If that's all you need, we're done. Send me the forms, I'll sign them and send them back, and then I don't ever want to hear from you or the rest of your family again."

"Come on, Celeste. Don't be so drastic."

"You're talking to me like I'm the same old Celeste I was before Marc died, but I'm not and I never will be again. I can't be. He broke me beyond repair, so now I'm taking the pieces and rebuilding myself into someone new."

"That's all well and good, but you don't have to—"

"Yes I do." It hurt to say the words, especially now that Lane had finally shown a spark of interest in repairing their friendship, but she had to do it. And the reason why was as clear and sharp as the winter sunlight outside her cabin. "I can't finish doing that if I'm still chained to who I was. This is me breaking those chains. Goodbye, Lane."

This time, it was with a deliberate gentleness that she ended the call and set the handset on the island counter. Her body quivered with the finality of that disconnect, and she took a step toward her work area, but her legs gave out long before she made it. She crumpled to the floor as tears spilled from her eyes, silent but not as unfeeling as those she'd cried so many times. Somewhere deep inside, grief welled, agonizing over the senseless loss of a friendship. Maybe there would come a day when she could try to build a bridge to Lane, but she doubted it. There was too much truth in her goodbye. If she had any chance at rebuilding herself, she couldn't have any ties at all to what had destroyed her in the first place. Not even the beneficial bond of friendship.

Bard wormed his way into her arms, and she buried her face in his soft black fur, glad for his empathetic and ever-present companionship but wishing with a surprising need that Brodie was here already.

That desire in itself was enough to stop her tears and push her off the ground. The peace her painting had brought her was well and truly shattered, but she started preparations for dinner, and the task was enough to shut the pain away again. She went about her work with the same deliberate motions with which she'd ended her final call to Lane and refused to think of anything but the chopping and mixing of ingredients. She'd made a rare find of fresh shrimp at the supermarket in Devyn yesterday, so she was making Diablo shrimp for Brodie. When she caught herself staring at the bottle of Riesling and felt the old dread beginning to crack her shield of numbness, she turned abruptly away and stepped outside for a moment, hanging in the open door of the mudroom and letting the biting air and first golden bloom of sunset wash through her senses. How long would it be before she could look at a bottle of wine or brandy or bourbon or even beer and no longer shudder or want to vomit?

While she was catching her breath, Brodie pulled up. A shy smile burned away the numbness and shiver of dread, and she curled her bare toes around the edge of the doorsill as she waited for him to reach her. In his hand, he clutched a bouquet of flowers—not the typical red roses of passion but rather red and yellow tulips and a stem of wisteria. Was the message intended or accidental? Because the flowers were a declaration of being hopelessly in love and a promise of steadfast commitment. She didn't feel brave enough to ask.

"You didn't have to bring me flowers," she murmured. "Believe me, Brodie, you don't need to woo me. But thank you."

"Who says I'm trying to woo you? I thought we were past that point."

"I guess we are. Come on in."

He gave her a quick kiss on the cheek as he stepped past her into the mudroom. She waited while he kicked off his boots and hung his coat on one of the hooks above the bench. She loved that feature of this cabin, and whenever she got around to buying her own place, she wanted one in it even if she had to build it herself.

"How was the ski hill?" she asked once they were inside.

"Good. Busy."

Bard trotted into the kitchen as soon as he heard Brodie's voice and meowed for attention. Celeste smiled when Brodie indulged him. There weren't any vases in the cabin, so she pulled out the biggest, most stable glass, filled it with water and the plant food that came with the flowers, and settled them in it, then set them on the dining table.

"How was work for you today?" Brodie asked.

"I didn't do much. Finished up a cover and sent the proof off to the author… and then I painted for myself."

"Oh? Can I see?"

"Sure. It's over on the table by my desk."

While he inspected her latest painting, she returned her attention to dinner. She was still too shaky, and she didn't like the way her hands trembled as she chopped six cloves of fresh garlic and tossed them into the saucepan with a stick of butter and quarter teaspoon of cayenne pepper. She was relived Brodie was here, but at the same time, that relief pulled at her from the opposite direction as the tension from her phone calls with Lane. And there was still too much irritation lingering from her conversation with her mother, whom she hadn't yet called back. If she could just suppress those darker emotions and hold herself together long enough, she was certain Brodie's soothing presence would draw her fully out of them again. She dug the half-cup measuring cup out of the drawers along with the corkscrew and popped the cork on the wine. As she measured the wine out, Brodie finally commented on her artwork.

"This is stunning, lass. I think it's my favorite one yet." He paused, head tilted as he took in every line and color of the painting. "Interesting color choice for your rose. Creativity and potential melded with magic and majesty and love."

She set the bottle down and stared at him. "You know flower meanings? How?"

"A friend of mine owns the floral shop in Devyn, and to be honest, flower lore has always fascinated me. It's a family tradition Dad brought over from Scotland along with his Scottish Highland cattle."

"You are a very intriguing man, Brodie." She narrowed her eyes and pursed her lips as he glanced over his shoulder at her, and she noticed that he'd picked Bard up at some point. The cat had his paws over Brodie's other shoulder and was currently nudging the man with his nose, demanding that the petting be resumed. "You say I have layers, but I daresay you have a few of your own. I think I could spend my entire life with you and never find out everything that is within the scope of your interest."

"What can I say? I'm insatiably curious."

So he likely *did* know the meaning of the flowers he'd brought… but that still didn't answer the question of whether or not his selection was intentional. And she was still too chicken to ask, so she returned to her meal prep with a whole new collection of agitating emotions. When the butter was completely melted and bubbling lightly and the rich fragrance of the garlic and pepper filled the kitchen, she poured the wine into the sauce and turned up the heat, clipping the bottle with her elbow as she reached to set the measuring cup in the sink. It tumbled to the floor, sloshing wine all over the kitchen.

The fragrance of it curled around her, and she gagged as the memories forever bound to the smell of alcohol dug talons of ice into her. Tears burned her eyes in her effort to stave off the retching her stomach threatened, and she fumbled behind her for the paper towels. Brodie took them from her and mopped up the mess as best he could, then wiped up the rest with a damp rag. Still, the odor remained.

"No big deal, lass. It's not like either of us was planning to drink it, anyhow. Now, if it was milk you'd spilled," he added with a chuckle, "then we'd have a reason to cry."

It struck a nerve, and her frail grip on her emotions splintered. With an inhuman shriek, she knocked the measuring cup into the sink and whirled on him. "Can't you be serious for one goddamned minute?"

"What? You want me to be serious like your husband? He was *real* serious, wasn't he."

Brodie's expression hardened, and she would've taken a step back in shock if there had been anywhere to go. As it was, she was already backed against the counter, and panic threatened. But he made no move toward her, and after a moment, his expression softened again.

"That's what I figured."

His voice was so gentle that her heart ached to embrace it. Instead, she wilted to the floor for the second time in less than an hour. Brodie reached down, took her hand, and pulled her to her feet.

"Nope, I'm not going to let him beat you down again. Ever. You're done with him." He gripped her hand and rested his other against her waist to steady her until she nodded to let him know she could stand on her own. "You're going to finish cooking our dinner because I get the feeling you need something to do with your hands and because it burning would probably send you the rest of the way over the edge. And while you're doing that, you're going to tell me exactly what happened between you and him. We're to that point. I need to know, Celeste, because I can't help you without knowing what I'm up against."

Nodding, she put a pot of water on to boil, and when it was ready and the sauce was reducing nicely, she added the shrimp to the sauce and angel hair pasta to the water.

"I'm guessing he was an alcoholic since you have an unusually strong aversion to alcohol."

Again, she nodded.

"And the way you said Steph was lucky to have had a man who made her feel safe enough to go through that pregnancy leads me to believe he was the worst brand of asshole. Did he ever hit you?"

She shook her head, then stopped, tilting it back. "That's not true. He did the night he died."

"So, what? He yelled, screamed, broke things?"

"Mostly. He wasn't like that when we first got together, but just before we got married, he started drinking. Nothing major at first—a couple of beers after dinner. And he was supportive of my career. Of course, I figured out later it wasn't an interest in what I did for a living that spurred his support but rather a need to control me like he controlled everything else in his life." She stirred the shrimp, separated the noodles, and was glad to have the task to distract her. It made it easier, and she didn't doubt that

Brodie had known that. "The drinking…. His business was building, and he'd schmooze clients and contacts… only, it turned into worse, until he started getting drunk every night. He turned into a different person. When he was sober, he was charming and funny and you couldn't help but like him, but when he drank, he became this vicious, seething *thing*. Not human. Something less than human."

When the noodles were tender, she drained them, placed them into a bowl, and poured the shrimp and sauce over them. Normally, she would have tossed the noodles with olive oil and Parmesan cheese and served the shrimp and sauce on the side, but tonight, she didn't have the energy to be fancy. She wasn't hungry, either, but she started to set the table. Again, Brodie stepped in. He set the plates and silverware on the table and covered the pasta dish to keep it warm, then took her hand and led her to the couch. He didn't offer to hold her, leaving that decision to her, and with only a second's hesitation, she scooted close to him with her feet tucked under her and her knees resting on his thighs. Then she threaded her fingers with his and wrapped his arm securely around her. Bard, in his softhearted way, jumped up on the couch and curled up in her lap, purring and watching her with his bright blue eyes.

"I'm glad you don't seem to think I could ever be like him," Brodie murmured, petting the cat.

"I don't," she replied, surprised once again by the firmness of that belief. "I don't think a man like him could ever take in abused and abandoned animals or talk his son's mother out of an abortion because he so loved their baby even before he was born." She choked a little on that, but the surge of admiration and gratitude for Brodie prevented her from getting hung up on it. "Nor would he be able to do what you've done for me. You've helped me understand that I don't have to try to be who I was before. You've brought me back, Brodie."

"I'm glad."

"Besides, my cat adores you. He hated Marc."

Brodie scratched under the feline's chin, eliciting a contented purr.

"Do you think you would've left him if he hadn't died?"

The question was innocent enough, but it opened the door to a hurricane of fear and helplessness, and she shivered. "I'd like to think I would have, and I even tried… but I don't know that he would've ever let me."

"You feared for your life?"

"The night he died, after he hit me, he tried to strangle me." Her breath caught in her throat again, snagging on a trapped sob. "Because I…. Because…."

He tightened his arm around her, and she leaned into him as she tried to gather her courage. Marc had never done that. Even at the beginning, before he'd revealed his true nature, she'd never truly felt like he was there for her. He'd made her feel… alone. Maybe it was her innate independence that had blinded her to that; she'd never enjoyed having to rely on anyone but herself. But this was different. She wasn't relying on Brodie, but she knew he'd be there to catch her when she fell. And she would. There was no way she'd be able to get through this still standing on her own, not if she opened herself to it in a way she hadn't yet. When she'd told Shannon and Ty, she'd done it with a cold detachment—giving a report. But that wasn't going to help her. She needed to let it all out, face the emotions and consequences and let them wash through her. That was the only way she'd be able to clear away the broken shards of herself that couldn't, wouldn't, and shouldn't fit into the woman she wanted to build herself into.

"Back in June, that's when it got bad. I took a home p-pregnancy test. Even before I saw the results, I wanted it to be negative."

"Was it?"

She shook her head. "I suppose you could say that was the beginning of the end, because the thought that I couldn't put my child through what I endured before my mother left my father kept repeating itself over and over. I knew then, even before the positive showed up that I'd have to get away."

"That explains why you said Steph was lucky to feel safe enough to have Brendan. Or, I guess you said secure, but it means the same thing, doesn't it?"

Celeste nodded. "I debated all day whether or not to tell him, but when he came home half-drunk as usual, I couldn't do it. And then… then we fought because he needed me to model the clothing line he wanted to show at the Seattle Fashion Show, and I said no because I was just getting my cover design business started and there was a writers conference on the same day."

"How bad was it?"

"He destroyed my studio. All my work, my supplies, the orders for my Etsy store… everything. He broke windows. It took me a week just to clean it all up. In the morning, when he had sobered up, he apologized. He was back to being his charming self, but when he brought up the fashion show again, and I told him no again. He left the house, and when he came home hours later, he was drunk again. He yelled and screamed and broke glasses. Next morning, same deal. It went on like that for a couple weeks, but his apologies became less and less sincere. For the first time in my life, I began to consider an abortion. I never imagined I'd ever consider one in any case other than a danger to my life or some major birth defect." She choked on the words that followed. "I never thought the threat to my life would come from outside. After one really bad fight—almost as bad as the one that ended with my studio demolished—I left. I checked into a hotel because I knew he'd find me if I went to a friend's or my grandmother's."

Brodie stroked his hand over her head and down her arm, and she pinched her eyes closed, concentrating on the heat of his body.

"In the morning, when I opened the door to take my bag out to my car, he was standing there, stone sober. He offered no apology at all. And that's when I knew he'd never let me get away if he knew I was pregnant. He'd find me, no matter how far I ran or where I hid. That's when I made the decision to…."

She'd told Shannon and Ty, so why couldn't she say it now? She curled her fingers around Brodie's arm and dug them into the muscle until they ached, but he uttered no complaint. Tears threatened again, but this time, there wasn't merely a hint of the raw emotion that had until recently been encased in dark hollowness; there was a flood waiting for the slightest crack to form in the dam holding it back.

"I went home with him, and after he left for work, I

made an appointment to have an abortion. Two weeks later… I did it. I had to walk through a crowd of protestors yelling at me that I was a baby killer and that I was going to rot in hell for what I was doing."

"If only they'd known you were already in hell," Brodie murmured. "I'm so sorry, lass."

"I am, too. I wish I could say I wanted that baby, but I never had a chance to think about it. All I could think was that if I had the baby, I'd never get away from him, and if I didn't get away from him, I'd die. Either he'd eventually turn violent and kill me, or I'd end up dying young like Gran Sylvia with the life sucked out of me until there was no will to live left in me."

With a tiny squeak, the first tears started falling… the first *real* tears.

"Looking back, I know that if I'd had any hope at all that I could get us both away, I wouldn't have gone through with it. That day was the worst of my life. Even the night Marc died wasn't as horrible as that."

"What happened?"

"He found out about the abortion."

"How?"

"One of the protestors saw him in Seattle and recognized him. She'd recognized me at the clinic because I'd modeled some of Marc's clothes before. She called him a conspirator to the murder of an innocent baby and then told him she'd seen me go into the clinic."

"Holy hell."

"He wasn't drunk that night. He came home, I believe, with every intent to kill me. He confronted me about it, and I tried to tell him why, but of course, that was something he couldn't hear." Strangely, this part was easier to tell, perhaps because it offered justification for her fears or simply because it was difficult to feel both the grief over her child and the animalistic terror of that confrontation. "He hit me, split my lip open, and I ran. He caught me, hit me again, and that later turned into a black eye. The neighbors heard me screaming, I guess, and called the cops. The first showed up within minutes—a female cop and her rookie partner. They were on patrol nearby. By the time they broke down the door, Marc had chased me into the kitchen, and he had me pinned against the counter by the sink with his hands around my throat. The female cop was the first to reach us, and he hit her in the face with his elbow."

The image of the female officer's face, of the blood streaming from her nose, hit Celeste hard. The same guilt and self-loathing and worthlessness that had triggered the violent rage that night again crashed through her.

"He broke her nose. I heard it crack, and when I saw the blood—that's when I broke." She could still remember how that inhuman, gurgling shriek had burned her already aching throat and could still feel the squared grip of the chef's knife digging into her hand. That she'd managed to make any sound at all with his hand squeezing the life out of her was a miracle. "In that split second, I reached back for the knife on the counter… and I stabbed him. Jammed all six inches of the blade up under his ribs."

Brodie probably didn't want to hear the details, but she couldn't stop herself. The words were flowing now. She described the way Marc's eyes had sprung wide in surprise, the soft gasp he'd given, and the hot, sticky spurt of blood that trickled down the blade over her hand. She told him how she'd stood rigid against the counter long after Marc had slumped to the floor, how she'd still been frozen to the spot when the ambulance came, and how she'd finally fallen to pieces on the floor of that kitchen blubbering an apology to the cop whose nose Marc had broken after the EMTs had taken him away.

She was blubbering again now as the rest of the story tumbled out of her—her obligatory arrest, the ride down to the station, the long hours talking to the police, finding out that Marc had died on the way to the hospital, and the crippling fear and conflicting resignation and rightness that she was likely going to prison for his murder.

"But it was clearly self-defense," Brodie said with a touching note of indignation in his voice. "And the cops were there to see that."

"No charges were ever filed. The next morning, while I was waiting for Grandma Letty to come pick me up, I asked to use the restroom to make myself as presentable as I could. I noticed the dried blood in the ends of my hair, and that's when I cut it all off."

"How did you get scissors?"

"By that point, I had my purse back, and I had a small pair in it."

"You had a purse? I don't think I've once seen you carry a purse the whole time you've been here."

She sniffed and wiped under her eyes. "A lot changed that night." The derisive laugh came out as a choking sob. "Everything changed. I k-killed my husband because I was too weak to get away from him before I was backed into a corner I couldn't get out of any other way. And, oh my God, that baby…. I deserved to be locked away. I wish I had been."

"Hey," Brodie murmured. "Don't talk like that. You are many things, lass, but you are *not* weak, and you don't deserve to be locked away. Your life was in danger, and you reacted from the most basic instinctual drive—the will to survive. It's not your fault that you were pushed to that point."

"You don't have to be nice to me, Brodie. I know what I am."

"I'm not being nice, and you obviously *don't* know what you are. You are just like Charlie and Moon. When I first adopted them, they had known nothing but cruelty, so they ran and hid, and when they couldn't do that, they snapped and clawed. They had retreated into the most primal state of being. Animals and people in that state…. There is no room for anything but live or die, so they run, and when they can't do that, they fight. Because that's all they can do. And when they can't fight anymore, they give up and die. Like your Gran Sylvia." He lifted her into his lap and held her tightly, and when he spoke again, his voice was strangled. "Thank God you didn't reach *that* point."

That he saw value in her and wanted her was more than she could handle right now. The walls crumbled, brought down by a torrent of gratitude and grief, and for the first time, she allowed herself to feel it all. She clung to him and cried.

"That's it, lass," he whispered. "Let it out. You don't have to face it alone anymore."

Ten

AT LAST, DAYBREAK BRIGHTENED the interior of the A-frame cabin, and the features of the woman sleeping in Brodie's arms began to materialize as it grew. She'd finally settled down enough to eat just after ten, and even cold, the shrimp and pasta had been delicious with the spice adding plenty of heat. He'd called Ainsley shortly after that to ask her to check on his animals, let them out, and let them out again this morning. She must've noticed something out of place in his voice because she hadn't joked about him spending the night with Celeste. Around midnight, he, Celeste, and Bard had curled up in bed together in the loft, and to Brodie's surprise, she'd fallen into a deep, healing sleep and hadn't woken once during the night. He knew she hadn't because he'd spent all the hours between then and now staring blindly into the darkness, assimilating it all.

"I guess she trusts me enough to protect her at her most vulnerable, eh, Bard?" Brodie whispered to the cat, who was curled up behind his knees. Bard regarded him with eyes narrowed in contentment. "I'm glad to see you still approve of this. Maybe we should introduce you to my critters and see how well you get on with them. I think you might be seeing a lot of each other soon."

He'd had plenty of time to digest everything and absorb the shock of it, and as day broke, the world righted itself, and that head-spinning surrealism of being caught between disbelief and certainty had lessened until he now felt like the ground wasn't tilted beneath him. Had he even been surprised? Not really. He'd been collecting clues since she'd arrived, and he'd been fairly certain of every detail except how her ex had died. That was the one piece of the puzzle he hadn't guessed and the one that maintained that phantasmagorical aura. He didn't like how clearly he could picture that scene or the primordial terror in her eyes. His heart had felt that emanating from her enough times to know every word she uttered last night was the truth.

Gently, he lifted a lock of hair that had fallen across her eyes and tucked it behind her ear. She was sure to ask if anything she'd told him would alter his opinion of her, so he'd better have an answer that would alleviate that fear without a shadow of doubt. He kissed her bare shoulder, then tucked his arm more tightly around her waist, pulling her into him. She stirred, curling her hands around his arm.

"Did you sleep at all?" she murmured.

"No, but that's all right. I needed to think more than I needed sleep."

She rotated in his embrace and searched his face with

wide eyes. Doubt and resignation turned them from the color of rich earth to shadowed onyx as she averted her gaze. "See?" she whispered. "I told you I'm broken. I told you you don't want to be with me."

"Still my decision, and I've decided that I *do* want to be with you—now more than ever. You forget that I have a giant soft spot for broken and mistreated things."

"I haven't forgotten."

"Good. Because I have a lot of work ahead of me to rebuild your faith in men, and I want to be sure you're going to stick around long enough for me to try."

"You believe me?"

"Of course I do."

"I could've made it up."

"Add liar to the list of things you are not, right up toward the top with weak."

"How can you be so sure?"

"A liar wouldn't let her heart and soul bleed out onto paper for the world to see like you did with that rose painting or with every piece of art you create. Besides, you're not smooth enough to be a liar. You're all sharp and sometimes brutal honesty wrapped in velvet compassion."

She was quiet for a while, and he sensed a contemplativeness about her. "Exactly how much did you figure out... and how?"

"How Marc died was the only blank I hadn't filled in, although now that I think about it, the clue was right in front of me. That first time I startled you, you were working on a cover with a bloody knife. Why'd you take that job on? Seems like a sure-fire trigger for that memory."

"That wasn't the original plan for the cover. It

evolved into that. What about the rest?"

"The abuse wasn't hard to figure out, either—your skittishness gave that away—and your unusually strong aversion to alcohol led me to believe whoever hurt you was an alcoholic. Steph thought you might've had an abortion or a miscarriage by a comment you made to her, and please don't be mad at her for telling me. She thought I should know so I wouldn't say something stupid and insensitive on accident. Because, well, you know me."

He hoped she would laugh or at least crack a smile, but she only searched his face with eyes wide and insecure beneath brows drawn together.

"Are you… okay with that?"

The hopefulness entwined with apprehension in her voice made his heart ache for her. "If you're asking if I think any less of you because of it, no, I absolutely do not."

"But I—"

"No, lass. I know what you're thinking, and I want you to stop it." He clasped her face and kissed each cheek before pressing a chaste kiss to her lips. "You made the only choice you could. Do you think that child would have survived without you? Marc tried to kill you the night he died. Who's to say he wouldn't have tried again and succeeded?"

She opened her mouth to contradict him, gulped as new tears wavered in her eyes, and finally pinched her eyes closed. A tear escaped between her lashes, and when she spoke, her voice quivered. "And what about Marc? I killed my husband, Brodie. How can that not freak you out?"

"Ex-husband," he corrected. "Let's get that straight right now."

"We were still married."

"Maybe so, but you were on your way out. And it doesn't freak me out because I've seen the damage he did to you. He'd still be alive if he had let you walk away like you tried." He tightened his arms around her again. "That's your first instinct. You're a fighter—you wouldn't have survived that if you weren't—but your first instinct is to flee. Correct me if I'm wrong."

She shook her head.

"I didn't think so. I may crack jokes when I shouldn't and make light of things that are serious, but I've always had a knack for gauging people, and when it comes to you, I know you have a heart as pure as the stars."

"You're not… afraid of me?"

"Why would I be? You're not dangerous. You have a line that flips the switch from flight to fight, just like any creature with a will to live, but fortunately for us both, I know exactly where it is and there's no chance I will ever get anywhere near it."

"No," she murmured. "I don't think it's possible you could."

"You think or you know?"

Her eyes popped open, and for a long while, she said nothing, only gazed at him with that heartbreaking vulnerability. Her hesitation might have been a sign of doubt in him, but he saw differently. It wasn't him she didn't trust but her own instincts. Then, with a subtle tilt of her chin, the doubt was gone.

"I know," she said firmly.

"Glad to hear it." Abruptly, he kissed her, then flipped the covers back and rolled out of bed. "Time to get up and greet a new day."

"Are you always so chipper in the morning?"

"I try to be."

To his astonishment and glee, a genuine smile brightened her face. "I could get used to that. I've always been a night owl, but I never used to dread the mornings like I have for the last… several months. The last year, really. I don't think I realized until just now how much I miss greeting the mornings like an old friend."

"You have such light in you, lass," Brodie murmured. "And I am deeply sorry Marc's shadow blocked it out."

Celeste slid out of bed, and Brodie glanced over her. She shouldn't look so sexy in those boxer shorts and loose, well-worn T-shirt, but *damn*. She'd been too distraught last night for him to pay much attention to her physical attributes, but that thin material left very little to the imagination. In the cool air, her breasts and nipples were taught, and it was impossible *not* to notice. And that graceful neck of hers, on display with that short hair…. It begged to be kissed and nuzzled. Beneath the hem of her shorts, her legs retained a hint of summer's tan, and the elegant lines of muscle were a testament to her enjoyment of physical activities. And he bet her skin was as soft as could be. *Jings, crivens, an' help ma boab. You gotta stop thinking like that, Brodie.*

With a low groan, he averted his gaze before he forgot why begging her to make love to him right now was a terrible idea.

"Have you thought of growing your hair out again?" he heard himself ask.

"I've tried a couple times, but every time I do…."

"You end up back in that police station bathroom

where you chopped it off," he surmised when it became apparent she wasn't going to finish the thought.

"I miss having long hair, though. Maybe I'll be able to grow it out if I try again."

"You know, as much as I usually prefer long hair on women, I actually like the short hair on you. It suits you in a lot of ways." He turned around to face her again, and mercifully, she'd pulled on a plain black hoodie. He combed his fingers back through her hair, pleased when her eyes slid closed and she leaned into his touch. "It shows off your neck, and it gives you this air of defiant confidence, which, for some reason I can't explain, I find incredibly sexy."

"You do, do you?" She angled her body against his and threaded her arms around his neck, pressing her breasts against him in a tantalizing way that made his heart pound.

"Yep. Distractingly so. It reassures me that you'll come back from this even stronger than you were before."

"Oh?"

The intent was plain in her chocolate eyes, and heaven help him, he wanted to take her up on that blatant offer more than he'd wanted anything in a long time. He recognized a glint of that to-hell-with-it attitude, but it was subdued, outshined by authentic desire. When that hunger had burned away the last traces of the recklessness, then he'd take her up on her offer. But not until then. Still, he couldn't resist playing with fire, so he lowered his head and found her lips waiting.

The woman could kiss. She teased him playfully one second, submitted to him the next, and then took command with such assertiveness that he'd have no chance of keeping his head if he hadn't spent all night thinking of the reasons why she'd cried herself to sleep in his arms.

When she slid her hands up the bare skin of his torso from his navel all the way to his collarbones and around his neck before burying them in his hair, he gently pulled away, careful to show her that he was reluctant to do so.

"As good as it would feel to keep going all the way to the end," he whispered, "I think you know as well as I do that right now is *not* the time to go for it."

"Thank you."

Not quite the response he was expecting. So he asked, "For what?"

"For caring about what's best for me."

"Believe me, lass," he murmured, kissing her lightly again, "it is my pleasure."

They headed downstairs, and Brodie stoked the fire while Celeste made breakfast. He started to tell her she didn't need to do that, but thought better of it, figuring the methodical task would help settle her mind again. He asked to use her phone and called his sister.

"Dogs have already been out," Ainsley informed him. "Cats are fed. How's Celeste?"

"Better, I think."

"Good. What happened, if I may ask?"

"I got the whole story."

"How bad?"

"Bad."

Ainsley sighed audibly. "You think she'll ever get over it?"

"She already is."

"You think you guys'll—"

"Thanks for taking care of my animals," Brodie said

abruptly.

"Hey, don't get all defensive on me. I like her, you great big turd. A lot. Enough that I'd like to have her as a sister-in-law. And don't even try to pretend like you haven't thought about it."

"Let's just wait and see what happens, all right?"

She responded by blowing a raspberry.

"Love you, too, sprite."

Chuckling, he ended the call and joined Celeste in the kitchen, skimming his fingertips over the nape of her neck before pressing his lips to the curve of her shoulder.

"I'm guessing that was Ainsley," she murmured.

"How'd you guess?"

"There aren't too many other people I would call a sprite."

"Hmm. Good point."

"Did she ask why you stayed over?"

"Of course. Just like any playful woodland sprite, she has an insatiable curiosity coupled with a tendency to stick her nose where it isn't welcome."

Celeste laughed softly. "I don't mind. I like your sister."

"The feeling is mutual, and she made sure to point that out. Anyhow, are you still up to coming to Butte with me in a little bit to get Brendan? I'll understand if you aren't."

She plated their breakfast—simple but satisfying grilled chicken, onion, green pepper, and cheddar omelets—before she turned to him, frowning. "I want to go," she said slowly, "but no, I don't think I'm up to it today. I'm sorry."

"No need to be sorry, lass. I didn't figure you would be. Do you mind if I bring Brendan over this afternoon? He'll be disappointed if he doesn't get to see you. Maybe, if you're up for it, we can all hit the slopes."

"That would be wonderful," she replied. An exquisite, soft smile gentled her features, and he couldn't think of a moment when she'd looked more attractive. "I really enjoyed my one-on-one time snowboarding with him the other day. You have an amazing son, Brodie. He's already as big-hearted as you are."

"He enjoyed it, too. He hasn't stopped talking about it since, which is what made me think a little skiing or snowboarding this afternoon might be good for us all."

"Thank you. Again."

"For what?"

"For everything. For helping me through this, for sharing your son with me and letting him fill that void for me. For just being… you."

"Well, damn. This is the first time I've ever been thanked for being my obnoxious, nosy, cracking-jokes-at-the-wrong-time self. You must have really low standards, lass."

"I'd like to think that I have pretty high standards. Marc was an asshole, but he was also successful, motivated, and handsome. And you have him beat in a couple essential areas."

"Let's see. For one, I'm not an asshole, right? What's the other one?"

"You're definitely not an asshole, but I was thinking more that you are as far from that side of the spectrum as it is possible to get. You have everything he had—success, motivation, attractiveness—*and* you're a devoted father and one of the most understanding friends I've ever had… right when I needed one."

"You have Shannon."

"Yes, I do. But I was so screwed up that even she couldn't save me."

He tilted his head and studied her with his eyes narrowed long enough that she squirmed beneath his gaze.

"What?" she asked.

"You said *was*. Past tense."

She opened her mouth to dismiss his remark, then snapped it closed and stared at him as his meaning sank in. He didn't give her a chance to think too much about it and kissed her passionately to drive it from her mind.

When they were sitting down to breakfast, he asked, "Have you ever considered talking to Pat about Marc?"

Frowning again, she hesitated before she answered. "I didn't meet him until after he married Aelissm, so I keep forgetting about his ex." Her lips twitched. "Shannon still calls her the Bitch."

"It's a fitting term. So is demon spawn from hell."

"You met her?"

"Not really. I was at the potluck when she came out here—that was the day she died. To this day, I still have no idea how a man like Pat ended up with a woman like that." Brodie paused. "Probably the same reason a woman like you ended up with a man like *your* ex. You're both gentle souls too willing to accept the bad in someone in the hope that the good will outshine it. Anyhow. Think about talking to Pat when he and Aelissm get back from Washington in a couple weeks. He could probably give you a whole lot better perspective than I can since he's been where you are, and I think you're probably to a point now that you *can* talk about it, since, you know, you just spilled the whole jar of beans to me last night. Am I right?"

She nodded.

He didn't let her bring it up again while they ate and cleaned up after breakfast, but the thought occupied him all the way to Butte. Funny how many drives to pick his son up had been spent daydreaming about the shaken, confident brunette who had breezed into his life like the best part of the sweetest dream.

"No Celeste today?" Stephanie asked when she answered her door. "Uh-oh. Trouble in paradise?"

"Not at all. We had a good long talk last night, and she wasn't feeling sociable."

"Ah. I'm going to go out on a limb and guess that she did most of the talking."

Having heard his father's voice, Brendan bounded into the living room and hurled himself at Brodie, who scooped him up and hugged him tight. While he didn't feel so lonely or so anxious on the weekends when Brendan was with his mother—that was all Celeste's doing, captivating him so thoroughly as she did—relief flooded through him, and the sensation that all was right in the world snapped back into place.

"Missed you," he whispered.

"Missed you, too, Papa." Brendan leaned back in his father's arms and glanced around the living room. "Where's Celeste?"

"She didn't come today."

"How come?"

The disappointment was a palpable cloud that descended on him, and it both squeezed and lifted Brodie's heart. He explained in simple terms his son was sure to understand.

"But she wanted to, didn't she?"

"Of course she did. And that's why I need you to hurry. We're all going to go skiing when you and I get home."

"Really?"

"Yes, really, so go get your stuff."

Brodie kissed Brendan's cheek and set him on the floor, then watched with his hands tucked in his pockets as the little boy raced back to his room with an ear-to-ear grin.

"So… was I right about her?" Steph asked.

"Yes, and I'm glad you told me. That heads up gave me plenty of time to think about it, so this morning when she asked me if I thought any less of her, I could say with honesty that I don't."

"That's good, Brodie. What about the rest?"

"She's been through hell, and I am amazed at how well she's bouncing back. She's incredible."

"Sounds like it. Brendan adores her. He's talked non-stop about their ski day all weekend, and from what I gathered, she loves him as much as he loves her." Steph slipped her hands around his upper arm and settled her head on his shoulder. "She'll be a good mom to him. Much better than I am."

"You're a good mom, Steph. Even better for the fact that you never wanted to be one, so I wish you'd stop saying things like that. Do you have any idea how much it bothers me?"

She planted herself in front of him. "First of all, Brodie, I wasn't belittling myself this time. Secondly, if you think I'm a good mom and I say she'll be better than me, logically that means she'll be a great mom, right? You'd better put a ring on her finger quick." She poked him in the chest. "Before you chase her off with your constant wisecracks."

"She's not ready for that yet, and I don't know how long it will be before she is."

"So?"

"Papa doesn't joke with her as much as he does with other people," Brendan interjected, dragging his overnight bag behind him as he joined them in the living room again.

Stephanie spun on Brodie with brows lifted. "Then she's *definitely* a keeper."

"Oh?" he inquired flatly.

"Yeah. With her, you're free to take the situation as it is rather than needing to find the brighter side because *she* is the brighter side."

That statement stuck with him all the way back to Northstar, and even Brendan's excited chatter about hitting the slopes with Celeste couldn't distract him from it. *Nail, meet hammer.*

As her name hinted, Celeste was a star that had been encased in a thick black shell, but now cracks were forming, and the light was beginning to shine through… the brightest, purest light Brodie had beheld since Inez's light had gone out. Maybe even brighter, because Celeste was harvesting fuel and strength from the darkness that had enshrouded her.

Eleven

CELESTE TWISTED HER GLASS of iced tea around with her fingertips and watched over her shoulder as Pat waved farewell to the guests who'd stopped in for a quick lunch after they'd checked out of their room. He locked the main door of the Bedspread Inn's restaurant and returned to the bar where she sat. He picked up a rag that smelled strongly of bleach and wiped down the bar.

It had been surprisingly easy to tell him every detail about her relationship with Marc, partly because she'd already revealed it to Brodie, partly because of his friendship with Bill Granger—who had, as lead detective for the Kitsap County Sheriff's Department, been the one to oversee the investigation—and partly because he exuded a gentleness that made her feel safe.

"Until recently, you and Bill Granger were the only men in my life who've been in it for more than a minute and haven't ever hurt me in some way or another," she said, resuming their conversation right where they'd left it before his customers had interrupted to pay.

"Until recently?"

With a will of their own, her lips lifted. "Ty and Brodie haven't hurt me yet, either."

"There is no *yet*, my dear. They won't ever."

Pat paused in his task and studied her with eyes narrowed.

"You already know that," he observed. "You just don't believe it yet."

"I'm starting to. I don't doubt Brodie. I *know* he's a good man."

"Then what's the hang up?"

"I come from a long line of women who make stupid decisions about men. My mother and both grandmothers."

Pat dunked his rag in the bucket of bleach water and wrung it out, then resumed wiping the bar top as he listened.

"Gran Sylvia married a man who drove her to an early grave. And my mother seems determined to follow that same path. She only left my dad because of me, and she won't admit it, but I *know* she moved back to California to be closer to him. Even after all those years and what he did to us."

"I thought she was with someone else."

"She is. And he's not much better."

"What about your Grandma Letty?"

"She made a promise to herself that she'd never marry again, and to my knowledge, she never dated, either. She learned how to rely on herself and do everything for herself."

"She sounds like a strong woman to me, and that's the impression I got the couple times I've met her."

"She is."

"Let me get this straight. You've found a good man, you know he's a good man, and you want to keep him around… but you're still afraid you're going to make the same mistakes the women in your family have made. That doesn't make much sense."

She laughed. "No, I guess it doesn't. Unless I do something stupid like dump him because I have the same instinctive need to reject what's good for me that my mother has."

"I don't know many people with that instinct who have had either the drive or the idea to use their talents to build their own businesses from scratch. Doing something like that takes guts, and guts don't usually allow one to accept that defeatist mentality. Besides, I know you don't have it because you'd started the process of leaving. You made arrangements to rent the house you and Shannon shared, and you were supposed to move in on your birthday."

Celeste stared at him. She hadn't told him that tiny detail, not because she'd intended to keep it from him but because it had slipped her mind—an inconsequential footnote to the body of the text of those horrific months. "How did you…?"

"Shannon told me. And I'd bet a large sum of money that you would've done just that and to hell with Marc if he hadn't come completely unhinged the night before. You were planning to get out of that mess, and you know it."

"I.…" She folded her hands in her lap and stared at

them with unfocused eyes. "I'm not sure I would have gone through with it. I'm not sure he would've *let* me."

"I beg your pardon, but that's bullshit." He braced his hands on the bar in front of her, and when she looked up, his smile was gentle and understanding, contrasting his response. "It's perfectly natural to doubt your judgment after what you've been through. My relationship with Sara made me doubt mine, too. That's what abuse does to a person." He glanced over his shoulder into the kitchen, and his smile shifted to one of gratitude and affection. "I can beat myself up about how long I was with her, but the fact of the matter is that I ended it. And just like me, you can waste energy on the what-if scenarios, or you can admit that you were strong enough to say you were through suffering."

"It sounds so wonderful and admirable when you say it like that," Celeste murmured.

"It's admirable because it's the truth. Have I ever showed you this?" Pat tugged on the collar of his long-sleeved T-shirt to reveal a thick white scar under his collarbone. "That was my parting gift from Sara. She didn't like the idea of me leaving, so she stabbed me."

Celeste lowered her gaze from Pat's scar and turned her glass around a few more times before taking a sip to quench her suddenly dry throat.

"Oh, no you don't," he said quickly. "You are not Sara in this comparison."

"Except that I stabbed Marc just like she stabbed you."

"Marc was trying to kill you, Celeste, because he realized you were leaving. He could no more let that happen than Sara could let me leave."

Aelissm, who had been in the kitchen singing along to the stereo, joined her husband behind the bar. Teasingly, she asked, "Can you imagine how embarrassing it was for him? Here we have this big, tough cop, and Sara was a pint-sized spitfire."

"I'm sure it was just awful," Celeste replied, playing along. Aelissm's teasing, which obviously didn't bother Pat one bit, made her squirm. The memories of terror and abuse and of jamming the chef's knife into Marc were still too fresh for her to shrug them off so easily, but the fact that Pat could gave her hope that she'd someday get to that point, too. "But big, tough cop though he might've been, Pat has one of the gentlest souls I've ever encountered. I can see how someone as cruel and calculating as Sara could've used that against him."

"People on the outside ask why we didn't remove ourselves from the situation sooner," Pat said, "but it's never as easy as simply walking away."

"No, it isn't," Celeste agreed.

"Thankfully," he continued, pulling his wife into his arms with a faint, poignant light in his eyes, "there are plenty of people who either understand or who don't need to understand to help us see that we're not the faulty ones."

Celeste's face warmed and she had to look away when Pat kissed his wife with an unrepentant passion. After a moment, she returned her gaze to them, catching a moment of private appreciation of one another, like the other was the reason their heart beat. That right there. That's what her grandmother had wanted her to look for and to see. That was real love. What she'd had with Marc, what her mother had had with Celeste's father, and what her grandmothers had been embroiled in—none of that was love. It was one half's need for control and dominance finding fertile soil in the other half's desire to be needed and valued.

"Sorry you had to see that," Aeli said with a grin that said she wasn't sorry at all.

"I may not be used to seeing that kind of shameless affection, but it's reassuring."

"Anyhow, I'll let you two get back to your chat so we can all get out of here and dive into our New Year's Eve plans. You have some, don't you, Celeste? If not, you're more than welcome to join us and the Conners since Shannon and Ty haven't made it back from Washington yet."

"Thank you for the invitation," she replied, "but I promised Brodie and Brendan that we could play in the snow after dinner and maybe have a fire out in the yard. I know it's not much of a plan, but it's better than last year, watching Marc and his buddies get shitfaced at the party I spent days organizing."

"Playing in the snow sounds infinitely preferable," Pat remarked. "And anyone in Northstar will probably tell you that the simplest celebrations are often the best."

Aelissm stood on her toes to give her husband a peck on the cheek, then turned toward the kitchen.

"Hey, Aeli?" Celeste called.

"Hmm?"

"Thanks for letting me steal your husband away from his duties for a while."

"You're welcome." Aeli winked. "He's a pretty great guy, isn't he?"

"Yes, he is."

"Ah, shucks, ladies. You're going to make me blush."

"I don't think that's possible anymore, my love. You've lived with me too long."

Pat chuckled as his wife disappeared. While he cleaned and restocked the bar, counted the till, and started wiping off the tables, they talked about how he and Aelissm had gotten together. Celeste knew most of the story, but the way he told it added a wholly different hue, and as he talked, strokes of hope tinted her thoughts. Sara had been a vindictive, evil bitch, and while Celeste was certain it wasn't Pat's intention to point out that most of Marc's demons stemmed from the alcoholism, it was impossible not to see it that way. In the long run, it might make him easier to forgive, and though she was still a long ways from doing so, she would need to in order to completely forgive herself.

"Do you think you'll ever forgive her?" she asked abruptly.

"I did a long time ago. I couldn't truly let go until I did."

"That's what I figured." Celeste let out a breath, and with it went the tension that had gripped her throughout much of her discussion with Pat. Impulsively, she hugged him. "Thank you," she whispered, her words muffled by his shirt.

"You're welcome. It gets easier, sweetheart, I promise. And before you know it, you'll look back on this time and believe without a single doubt that you are resilient." He brushed her hair back from her face in the same way she'd seen him flip his sister's ponytail over her shoulder, and in that moment, gratitude for her honorary big brother swamped her. If she'd had a male role model like him growing up like Shannon had, it was possible she would've seen right through Marc and never said yes to him when he'd asked her out.

Stubbornly, Celeste straightened her spine. *No more what-ifs.*

"One more piece of wisdom before you go," Pat said. "We can't change what's happened, and even if we could, everything that we do and that happens to us makes us who we are. You can let all the bad things drag you down, or you can make them work for you and come out stronger for them. That choice is yours."

It was so well rehearsed that it couldn't be a spontaneous statement. "Who said that?"

"Our friend June."

"Wise woman."

"Very. Tell Brodie and Brendan hi from us."

"I will. Thanks again, Pat."

"You're welcome again."

She bid Aelissm farewell and headed for the still-unlocked side door.

"Oh, and Celeste?" Pat called. She turned to face him. "Happy New Year."

The way he held her gaze added depth to what was, on the surface, an ordinary felicitation. She nodded in acknowledgement and strode out the door.

Yes, I think it will be a very happy New Year.

Back home in her A-frame, Celeste sat on her couch and gazed out the windows at the stunning vista beyond. The restlessness was gone; she felt no gnawing need to fill the time until she headed down to Brodie's with work. At any rate, she was ahead of schedule on all her current projects. In this tranquility, she was free of the doubts and fears and memories and the terrifying numbness that had tightened every nerve and muscle in her body. They had served the purpose of preventing her from collapsing into that emptiness, but now there was no void, and in in the absence of those things, she was strangely fluid and weightless.

So weightless that she found herself rising to her feet. There was no burden to push her down into the cushions of the couch anymore.

It was too much to hope that it was gone for good, and she was wise enough to understand that there would still be bad days and worse moments, but the hope that now filled the void guaranteed she'd be able to pull herself out of the darkness.

While she waited for the time to pass, she painted. The redwoods and the amethyst-tipped lavender rose had been her first steps toward reclaiming her passion for her art, but this was something else. It was pure, undimmed abandon, and as the scene came to life, understanding dawned.

She was home.

This wasn't the kind of home made with a floor, walls, and roof, nor was it the kind of home painted by the loving brush strokes of family and friends. This was a home created by accepting who she was and forgiving what she'd done.

Thinking of the words June had offered to Pat and he in turn had offered to her, Celeste abandoned her painting for the time being and grabbed a notecard and her brush pens from her desk drawer. She decorated the card with the Northstar Mountains and a cozy cabin with glowing windows beneath a starry sky—a miniature version of her much larger painting, but with a tiny difference. She added the silhouette of a man and a woman and a little boy, all holding hands. The woman's free hand was outstretched toward a silvery wisp of a child.

"Forgive me," she whispered.

Then she penned her newest motivational message in glittery gold.

I choose to be stronger.

Just as she tacked it to the frame of the front door—she'd leave the one Brodie suggested at the back door—her phone rang.

"Hello?"

"Do I need to send Search and Rescue?"

Brodie. Her lips curved. "No. Why?"

"It's almost five, and you said you'd be down by three."

"It's that late already?" She glanced at the clock on her iMac. "Crap. I'm sorry. I guess I lost track of time."

"I figured it was something like that. Work or play?"

"Play."

"Good. I take that to mean your talk with Pat went well."

"It was great, but I'll tell you about it when I get down there. See you in a few."

"Sounds good. Hey, bring Bard with you."

"Why?"

"It's time we see how well he and my crew get along, don't you think?"

"I suppose so."

She ended the call and located her cat, who was still sitting on her desk where he'd sat while she painted. "What d'you think, Bard? Are you ready to meet some new friends?"

He blinked at her.

"Guess we'll find out. C'mon, big boy."

After she pulled her boots and coat on, stoked the fire and turned off all the lights but the Christmas lights still around the front windows—the tree had come down two days ago—she picked Bard up, draped him around her shoulders, and stepped out the front door.

The air was crisp but not *too* cold and held a faint promise of spring. It was below freezing, but barely, and while the sky was crystal clear, the dampness on the westerly breeze hinted at snow sometime in the next couple days.

It wasn't quite five, but the sun was still up, riding low over the southwestern ridges. With the winter solstice now over a week past, the world was slowly returning to the light, and the symbolism spoke to her. Once upon a time, she'd celebrated the solstice, but that was something Marc had driven her to suppress. Something told her that if she mentioned it to Brodie, he'd encourage her to take it up again. He might think it was silly or archaic, but he seemed to want her to indulge in what made her happy regardless of what he thought about it purely because it made *her* happy. Like her choice to keep beef and pork and factory-farmed poultry from her diet. He was the son of a rancher, and he certainly had no qualms about her preferences. For a man who liked to joke about everything, he hadn't once teased her.

Because he respects me as I am. That feels incredible.

Bard rode on her shoulders all the way down to Brodie's house, utterly unconcerned. When Brodie opened the door at her knock and his dogs bolted outside, Bard briefly dug his claws deeper into her shoulder. As soon as Brodie cooed his name, he relaxed and even meowed in greeting.

"He doesn't seem too concerned about the dogs," Brodie remarked, scratching under Bard's chin as Jake and Charlie bounced around them.

"He's been around dogs before. The people I got him from had two Newfoundlands, one of whom was a pup, and three screaming, bratty kids. They were friends of Marc's, and the husband brought Bard home as a kitten against his wife's express denial. We were over at their house the day Marc's friend brought him home, and I fell in love with him." She scratched under his chin and behind his ears and was rewarded with a loud purr. "And since the feeling was mutual, I brought him home with me when the wife threatened to take him to the humane society a couple weeks later."

"Sounds like you and he were the match that was meant to be in the first place. And the ruckus in that house certainly explains why nothing ever seems to ruffle him."

She nodded. "Moon and Binx might present more of a problem because he hasn't spent much time with other cats. Or they might not. I don't know."

"Let's find out, shall we? Besides, dinner is ready and Brendan has something to show you."

Before they headed inside, Brodie kissed her firmly with a hunger that let her know how much he'd missed her even though she'd seen him this morning. It was as wonderful to be missed as it was to be respected, and she relaxed into his arms, trusting him not to let her fall. Bard gripped her shoulders, and she laughed, reaching back to stroke him and reassure him.

"So? What's for dinner?"

"A smoked chicken with homemade barbecue sauce. And don't worry. I made sure I bought one that was cage-free."

Impulsively, she threw her arms around his neck and hugged him tightly, nearly sending Bard flying. The cat managed to hang on, but his tail whipped furiously, and he let out a small, concerned meow.

"Sorry, Bard," she murmured.

"What was that for?" Brodie asked. "I'm not complaining, mind you."

"You may be the most thoughtful and considerate man I've ever met. Or at least, the most thoughtful and considerate of me. Are you always going to be so kind?"

"That's the plan. Come on in."

As soon as she stepped through the door, she set Bard on the floor so he could nose around before Brodie let the dogs in. Brendan launched himself at her like he hadn't seen her in days instead of the handful of hours it had been. She lifted him off the ground, and when he wrapped his legs around her waist and his arms around her neck tight enough to choke her, she hugged him back, unable and unwilling to ignore the sense of *rightness*. If Brodie dropped to one knee right then and there and proposed with his son begging her to say yes, she'd have a damned hard time saying no even though she was in no way ready to entertain thoughts of marriage yet. Maybe it was her talk with Pat, the several talks with Brodie since she'd told him everything, or the impending end of the most tumultuous year of her life with the promise of a fresh page on which to paint a new, happier picture right around the corner. Whatever it was, the uplifting freedom that had flowed through her as she'd painted this afternoon was as strong as ever, if not stronger, even with the arms of a six year old threatening to break her neck.

A hiss and feline growling drew their attention into the living room. With Brendan still stuck to her like Velcro, Celeste followed Brodie in to see what commotion was stirring. His cats—the tailless white Moon and the black Binx—had just descended the stairs to notice an intruder in their home. Bard, in true Bard fashion, sprawled in front of the fireplace with his eyes slits of blue, his tail slowly tapping the floor, and only his ears laid back in a mild show of what could be considered disdain for the growling emitted by the two rescue cats.

The humans in the room stood still as statues as the pair stalked toward Bard. When he showed no reaction, they moved forward with increasing boldness until they were circling him with noses twitching. Bard rolled onto his back and gave them a look like, *Relax. Play.*

After Moon and Binx had sniffed him long enough to relax further, Bard shot off across the living room with his back and tail arched, batting at the cat and dog toys and brown paper scraps and art supplies scattered across the space. The other cats stared at him for a moment, but then they, too, were streaking through the house as if seized by a sudden and uncontrollable kittenish delight.

"Well, I'd say that went well. You have an amazing

cat," Brodie whispered. "And as I've found, pets are a good reflection of their owners. Brendan, why don't you go get your present for Celeste?"

Abruptly, Brendan dropped to the ground and raced upstairs. Celeste looked questioningly at Brodie, but he only grinned and strode to the back door to let the dogs in. All three cats immediately stopped their game when the dogs came in, but though Jake and Charlie were curious about Bard, they'd spent enough of their lives with Moon and Binx that the novelty soon wore off, and they sat at Brodie's and Celeste's feet, staring up at him with loving eyes and tongues lolling out the sides of their mouths.

A cascade of thumps announced Brendan's rapid journey down the stairs, and a moment later, he was standing in front of them, grinning broadly at Celeste with a slender package wrapped in a brown paper grocery sack and decorated with fire works and hearts and a wobbly "Happy New Year, Celeste."

A lump lodged in her throat as she took the present, and her vision wavered, distorted by a watery sheen.

"It's beautiful, Brendan," she murmured. "You did a great job on this. Even better than the wrapping you did for your dad's Christmas present."

"Thanks. You gonna open it now? Or do you want to wait until after midnight? Since it's a present for the new year."

She slid her finger along the seam on the back, briefly slipped it under the fold at the end with the intent to open it, then decided against it. By the feel of it, the way the paper sagged a bit an inch in from the sides, it was a picture frame. "I think I'd like to wait, but if you'd rather I open it now, I will."

"No, you can wait. That's okay."

"If it's all right with your dad—" She glanced at Brodie. "—I'd like to open it right at midnight… and I'm hoping you'll still be awake to help me."

"I don't know if he'll make it all the way to midnight," Brodie replied, "but I agreed to let him try this year."

"So, what are we gonna do first?" Brendan asked.

"We're going to eat dinner," Brodie replied. "Then we'll go start a fire in the fire ring."

Dinner was amazing, and Celeste was mildly surprised, though if anyone were to ask her why, she'd have no answer. Considering how adept Brodie was at parenting, running the ski hill, and "ramrodding" his construction crew in the summers—she believed him capable of the requisite attitude for that even less now than she had before—why wouldn't he be an efficient and perfectly capable cook, too? Perhaps it was only that she'd done all the cooking for them in the time they'd been together. Because, she realized with a start, he'd let her.

"Out of curiosity," she said idly as she dipped a piece of perfectly smoked chicken into a puddle of the mouthwatering homemade barbecue sauce, "since you're a pretty amazing cook, why have you let me do all the cooking until tonight?"

"It seemed like something you needed to do. Something you could control, a way for you to create when art was a struggle."

Yeah, I thought as much. "You know, all my life I've been told how hard I am to read. Even people who have known me for years say that, and yet you've been able to read me more easily than a picture book since day one. Why is that?"

"Because I didn't just look at your cover. I read the blurb on the back... and then I bothered to actually open the book. I think we can both agree that it's rather difficult to read any book if you don't open it, yes?"

"Agreed." She laughed brightly. "Spoken like a true bookworm."

"What can I say? I am what I am."

They lingered over their meal, laughing and joking, and Celeste *finally* played a full game of twenty questions with Brendan. He wanted to know about her art. How she'd gotten started, what were her favorite styles, what had made her decide to attempt to make a living at it, and she was amazed at the depth of his questions. Having known Brodie for a couple months now, she knew exactly where he got it from. Then it was her turn to ask the questions, and she asked about his mother, prodding carefully so as not to trigger any painful topics, and was again shocked at how easily and comfortably he answered. The picture he painted was of a little boy adored by both his parents—a gift to their lives even though he'd been unplanned. Guilt flashed momentarily, but she suppressed it. She would have adored her child, but with a conscious effort, she let go of that guilt. She didn't regret her choice; she regretted that she'd needed to make it.

It was a temporary release, but she couldn't let it or any of what had happened strangle the life out of her anymore.

After washing dishes together and cleaning up the kitchen and dining room, Brodie, Celeste, and Brendan headed outside to start a fire. The sunset had long ago faded, but the sky to the west was a vivid blue-green. The ridges of the West Northstar Mountains were black against it, and the lines of them were as sharp in the crystalline air as if they'd been carved with a scalpel. A slender, waxing crescent moon dangled above them, and a planet—Mars or Venus or Jupiter, she had no idea—gleamed brilliantly nearby. She inhaled sharply, awed.

Impulsively, she flopped on her back in the deep snow and flapped her arms and legs. Brendan joined her, and Brodie chuckled at them both while he got the fire going. As soon as the flames were devouring the wood, he too sprawled on his back in the snow. Then someone threw a snowball—Brendan was her first guess, but she wouldn't put it past Brodie—and their snow-angel-making session erupted into an all out snow battle. Somehow in the fray Celeste ended up Brendan's target. Brodie scrambled to her in an effort to shield her from his son's well-aimed snowballs, and he slipped, knocking her down with him. She let out a squeal before collapsing in laughter.

"That may be the most beautiful sound I've ever heard."

Giddy enjoyment shifted into tender affection, and she smiled up at him as he braced himself on his elbows above her. He beamed at her, then glanced up at the smudge of blue-green in the west and the ice-blue sliver of the moon.

"But, soft! What light over yonder mountains breaks?" he asked, gesturing westward with dramatic flair. "It is the east, and Celeste is the moon. Arise, fair moon, and kill the envious sun."

"Now we're changing Shakespeare quotes?" Her voice trembled with the giggles that still rippled through her. "And it's a crescent moon about to set in the west."

"Minor and inconsequential details." Returning his gaze to her, he briefly lowered his mouth to hers in a soft kiss. When he lifted his head again, his lips were twisted in a lopsided grin. "You *did* tell me once that if I wanted to impress you, Disney quotes wouldn't do it."

"For a man who never went to college, you have a shockingly broad vocabulary and are stunningly well read."

"As I've said before, I'm insatiably curious. Or maybe I felt the need to compensate for my lack of higher education." He kissed her again, whispering another quote from *Romeo and Juliet* against her lips. "If this is love, let me taste more of it."

She jerked her head back as far as the pillowing snow allowed and stared at him with wide eyes. "You love me?"

"Yes, I do. I think I've known it for a while, but you weren't ready to hear it. Now I think you are."

Before she could respond, Brendan piled on top of them, digging his mittened hands into the snow to give her a big hug. "I love you, too! Do you love me?"

"I absolutely do, little man. How could I not?"

"And my papa? Do you love him, too?"

With an arm pinning the little boy to her, she met his father's patient gaze, and her lips stretched in the widest grin that had graced her features in a long time. As she opened her mouth to reply, she felt her heart open, too, and peace and freedom and something she'd never fully tasted before rushed in, drowning her in the sweetest bliss, and she knew without a doubt that the words that flowed from her were the truth. "You bet I love your papa."

Suddenly, she wanted very much to know what photograph Brendan had chosen, certain that it *was* a picture like the one he'd given his father for Christmas, but she'd promised to wait until the clock chimed the end of this year and the start of the next.

That promise and the curiosity warred in her as she and Brodie and Brendan alternately chased each other around in the snow and warmed their chilled hands and faces at the fire, but around nine, it became clear that Brendan wasn't going to make it to midnight. He bravely fought his weariness and lasted until a quarter after ten, but when he nearly dozed off in Celeste's lap—they'd let the fire outside die down and moved inside to the couch to watch New York ring in the new year on TV—Brodie suggested it was time for bed.

"Aw, Papa," Brendan said through a yawn. "Can I try a little longer?"

"I suppose."

Brodie didn't ask Celeste if she minded holding the sleepy boy a little longer, and she liked that. It made her feel like she was already part of his and his son's life rather than a candidate still in the trial phase.

"But, just to be safe, maybe we should ask Celeste to open our present now instead of later."

Our?

Brodie grabbed the gift off the coffee table and handed it to her. Reaching around Brendan, she glanced at the handwritten "tag" the little boy had drawn into the corner of the paper and saw that the gift was not only from him but from his father as well. She glanced at Brodie, and he nodded encouragingly, so she carefully unwrapped the present, wanting to preserve Brendan's artwork; it was as precious as whatever it concealed.

"I know you still have a lot of work ahead of you, lass," he murmured, "but we wanted to give you something as a promise we'll be with you every step of the way."

More curious than ever, she slipped the picture frame from its wrappings—like the one Brendan had made for Brodie, it too was decorated with skis and snowboards— and sucked her breath through her teeth. She didn't remember Stephanie taking the picture, but she knew exactly when she had. They'd all gone skiing on Brendan's birthday back on the eighteenth of December, and Steph had snapped a picture of Celeste, Brodie, and Brendan piled together in the snow in a heap of skis, snow pants, parkas, knit hats, and smiles as wide as the Montana sky above them. Behind them, the lodge stood tall and proud. The tip of Brendan's ski had gotten lodged under a chunk of ice on their way to the lift, and he'd somehow taken out both his father and Celeste. When he'd started crying, worrying that he'd hurt Celeste, Brodie had wrapped them both in a bear hug, squeezing them until they'd laughed breathlessly.

"We look like a family," Brendan said with something akin to awe in his voice. He yawned again. "A real family with a dad *and* a mom."

"We do, don't we," Celeste agreed gently. "Thank you both so much for this."

"You're welcome," Brendan replied. Yawning yet again, he conceded the battle against sleep. "I think I should go to bed now."

"Go get changed, brush your teeth, and we'll be up

in a minute to tuck you in," Brodie said.

Without a word of complaint, the boy marched up the stairs, and moments later, the sound of a drawer opening echoed down. Brodie sat on the couch beside Celeste, shoving three cats out of the way. He chuckled when they immediately draped themselves over him and Celeste as if he hadn't just interrupted their snoozing. With an arm tucked around Celeste's shoulders, he dragged her against him.

"So, you love me," she said with a hint of amusement in her voice.

"I thought we'd established that already."

"We did. But I want to hear it again."

"I love you."

"So soon after Marc, that should terrify me. But it doesn't. It makes me feel…."

He gave her ample time to reply, but she couldn't seem to make herself say the word. Not because she doubted but because it dazzled her as thoroughly as the glittering stars strewn across the velvet night sky outside Brodie's cozy home, welcoming home.

"It makes you feel what?" he prodded quietly.

"Safe."

He clasped her face and kissed her tenderly, and she wrapped that sensation around her—the touch of his lips against hers, the gentle strength in the hands against her face, and the heat of his body that was so near and yet too far away.

"I love you, Brodie," she whispered. "You want to know what my New Year's resolution is? It's about you."

"In that case, I do indeed."

"To trust you and this. To believe that, even though I made a terrible decision once before in my life, I am making a good one now. I choose to be strong. I choose to believe I deserve happiness. And I choose to believe in you."

He kissed her again, then took her hand and helped her to her feet. They headed upstairs to tuck his son into bed, and the simplicity of reading a story to Brendan, of tugging the blankets up to his chin, and of checking under the bed to make sure there weren't any monsters was perfection. When she and Brodie leaned down to hug Brendan goodnight together and the little boy asked her for a kiss on the cheek, she hoped to have ten thousand moments more exactly like this.

Celeste left the room, and Brodie followed right behind, turning off the light on his way out. He left the door ajar.

They reclaimed their spots on the couch and snuggled together as the central time zone embraced the new year. Finally it was their turn. She and Brodie quietly counted down the last seconds of the old year, and when they reached zero, they kissed. Adoration and desire burned away the memories of the last year, and she sighed happily.

This is where I belong. A slow smile spread over her face and a fierce, determined love kindled in her heart. *This is home.*

Epilogue

"YOU MAY KISS YOUR BRIDE."

For the second time in her life, Celeste found herself waiting for a man to kiss her for the first time as her husband. The last time now seemed an eternity ago—a distant, unwelcome shadow in a neglected corner of her memory. Less than a year and a half removed, the shattered marriage that had begun with that first wedding kiss belonged to another life, a different Celeste. The Celeste Brodie now kissed with a dizzying combination of relief, joy, and impatience was a strong, independent woman who kissed her new husband back with equal fervor and without a trace of the shy trepidation that had tainted that first kiss. This Celeste was confident and proud and aware that she would never again feel that fear or pain because she wouldn't tolerate it. And because she'd found a good man who would never give her anything to be tolerated.

Around them, a small group of friends and family—her mother and grandmother, Shannon, Ty, and Jack, Brendan, and Brodie's parents, sister, and his Scottish uncle and grandparents—applauded and cheered the kiss that united Celeste and Brodie officially in marriage. The men all wore formal kilts of the Dunn family's tartan, and the women all wore that same sky-blue, yellow, white, and navy plaid somewhere in their attire. If someone had told her when she'd decided to take an extended trip to Northstar that doing so would be the start of a journey that would lead her all the way to a moonlit wedding on a farm in Scotland, she never would have believed it, yet here she was. Above her, a carpet of bright stars glittered, and around them, the flames of dozens of candles danced in the chilly ocean breeze. At the distant edge of the Dunns' farm, the ocean beat itself against the rocky cliffs, at once salting the air and moderating the winter chill that would have, back home in Northstar, made an outdoor wedding beneath the stars and brilliantly full moon on New Year's Eve a miserable affair instead of the magical event it should be… and was.

"Ya gonna kiss her again or what, lad?" the minister—Brodie's Uncle Fergus—inquired in a deep voice as powerful as the rest of him.

Brodie, whose gaze had like hers found the stars, chuckled and took her face in his hands. Dipping his head, he pressed his lips to hers and lingered long enough to elicit rowdy whoops from their friends and family. "I love you, lass," he whispered. "My light, my love. My wife."

"And I love you," she murmured. "Under the sun, under the moon, but most especially under the stars."

"Lads and lasses, it is my pleasure te introduce te ya fer the first time, Mr. Brodie and Mrs. Celeste Dunn."

Fergus's announcement was met with more cheering. So loud were the attendees of their small, private wedding that Celeste was glad there were no neighbors close enough to be disturbed by their late-night celebration. Brendan abandoned decorum and threw his arms around his father and his new stepmom. He had grown so much in the last year that Celeste was glad their lives hadn't crossed and intertwined any later than they had. As it was, she didn't have nearly enough time until he was grown and ready to spread his wings like the gulls still crying over the cliffs even this late into the evening. The thought awakened an ache she had stubbornly ignored this past year in order to focus on fully shedding the doubts and fears of her marriage to Marc, and she had planned to go on ignoring it for a while yet, but Brendan's first comment rekindled it into a blaze that she knew wouldn't be easily doused.

"So, when do I get a little brother or sister?" Boisterous laughter met his innocent inquiry, and he glanced at the adults around him in confusion. "What's so funny? It's not like Mom and Russ are going to have any kids, so that means it's up to Papa and Celeste."

"We'll see what happens, little man," Celeste said. "But don't get your hopes up in case it doesn't happen right away, all right?"

"But it *will*, right? You aren't going to be like Mom and say you don't want any kids, are you?"

Too quietly for anyone but Brendan and Brodie to hear, she said, "Thanks to you and your dad, no I'm not. But it's not like going down to the humane society and adopting a dog or a cat. It takes time."

"Yeah, nine months, right?"

Celeste laughed softly. "Sometimes a little longer than that."

"But Jack's going to get a little sister in April… and he's not even old enough to appreciate her yet!"

Celeste glanced sharply at Shannon, who hadn't yet told her what she and Ty had found out about their second baby's gender at their appointment the day before they'd all flown to Scotland. How had Brendan found out? She shoved that aside for the time being, and met her stepson's gaze. "I know you've already been waiting a long time, but I need you to be patient a little longer, okay? Can you do that for me?"

Solemnly, he nodded, and she stroked her fingers across his cheek and under his jaw before hugging him again.

"You're going to be a *great* big brother, Brendan."

"Thanks," he said more brightly.

As she walked up the short aisle and passed Shannon, she muttered, "I'll get you back for telling Brendan about your daughter but not telling me."

"I was waiting to tell you at your reception breakfast tomorrow because tonight is supposed to be all about you. Brendan only found out because he overheard Ty talking about names on the plane."

"Uh-huh. Sure. I know how persuasive my stepson can be." Celeste embraced her friend, then gave Ty a quick hug and smoothed her hand over Jack's silky hair before kissing the toddler's cheek and continuing up the aisle along the short line of well wishers to her mother and grandmother.

Dawn and Letty embraced Brodie first, welcoming him to their family.

"Thank you for making our Celeste so happy," Letty said, giving him a strong hug.

"Believe me, Grandma Letty, she's brought just as much happiness to my son and me, if not more. Excuse me a moment. Uncle Fergus is making a fool of himself trying to get my attention."

Sure enough, the hulking older brother of Brodie's father was nearly dancing in place trying to get Brodie to come over. The sight of such a big man, clad in a formal kilt, hopping and waving with his eyes bright was comical, and Celeste laughed.

"You've done it, my girl," Letty said, hugging her tightly before pressing a kiss to each of her cheeks. "I knew you would. And here we are *in Scotland* at your wedding. A fairytale come true for my fairytale girl."

"What have I done?"

"Broken the cycle," Dawn murmured.

Celeste eyed her mother warily. Their relationship was still strained, but that would mend in time, too, and as Celeste wrapped her arms around Dawn, she decided that should be one of her resolutions for the coming year.

"Hug me a little tighter, will you? I'd like some of whatever it is you have to rub off on me."

The laughter that tumbled out of Celeste surprised her, and she did as her mother asked. "Well, you've already taken the first step."

"I have?"

"Yeah. Walking away from that jackass you were

dating *before* it turned violent. I'm glad you listened to me, Mom. You already seem happier."

"I am," Dawn agreed. "And you, my daughter…. I don't think I've ever seen *you* so happy. You deserve every drop of it and more. So I'm going to give you one more hug and let you get to it."

With a wink, Dawn hugged her daughter, took Letty's hand, and wandered off to talk with Brodie's family, leaving Celeste alone to watch the two families mingle. Brodie came to stand beside her, chasing away the night's damp bite when he wrapped her in his arms.

"How's it feel to be married again, Mrs. Dunn?"

"Infinitely better than the first time. So much better, in fact, that I'm not sure the first time should even count anymore."

"Let's agree, then, that it doesn't. It's a chapter from a book we've burned." He kissed her with breathtaking demand and passion wrapped in understanding.

"Is it time to tell everyone good night yet?"

"Almost."

She beamed up at her husband. "I'm not going to take no for an answer from you tonight, my love."

"Good. Because I couldn't ask for another rain check tonight even if it wasn't our wedding night."

Celeste laughed as he twirled her away from him and back into his arms. Without letting go of her, he called his son over.

"You be good for Nana and Granddad tonight."

"But, Papa! How come I can't stay with you and Celeste in the cottage? It's our first night together as a family!"

"If you want a brother or sister, you'll stay with your grandparents, and you'll be a good boy for them."

Brendan glanced at Celeste with hope in his eyes, then joined his grandparents, half-sulking. Fergus's daughters, who had not attended the ceremony, pulled up in the car Brodie and Celeste were using during their stay at the Dunns' farm. Both were as spritely beautiful as Ainsley, favoring their fine-featured mother rather than their stout father.

"The cottage is ready for the newlyweds whenever they're ready for it," the older announced.

"Is it that time already?" Shannon asked.

"What do you mean *already*?" Celeste retorted to much chortling.

"Har har. Brodie, you are both the worst and best influence on her."

"I'm going to ignore the 'worst' in your comment because I happen to think jesting is an admirable skill to have."

Shannon rolled her eyes, but she was grinning.

Under a shower of lavender rose petals tossed skyward by their wedding guests and cries of *fáilte*, Celeste and Brodie jogged to their car.

Since they'd had the hair-brained idea to have a night wedding, no reception would follow immediately after the ceremony, and it felt a little odd to escape to their honeymoon cottage without that celebration. Tomorrow, she reminded herself. Tomorrow was for celebrating with their family, beginning with a breakfast to which Brodie's entire extended family as well as their neighbors had been invited, and for exploring this magical place Brodie's family had called home for generations. Celeste looked forward to all of it, but tonight was for her and Brodie, a chance to finally explore each other's bodies as thoroughly as they'd already explored each other's hearts and souls.

The drive across the farm to the stone cottage atop the cliffs took no more than five minutes, but it was too long. Anticipation hummed through her body, and as soon as Brodie parked the car in the front of their temporary home, she grabbed him by the chin and kissed him. If she weren't afraid to damage the delicate lace overlay of the gown Brodie's mother, grandmother, and great-grandmother had all worn to marry their Dunn men, she would've straddled him right there in the car.

"How about we wait until we get into the cottage and do this right?"

"Brodie," she responded huskily, "I long ago stopped being afraid that anything between us could ever be wrong."

"Let's not argue semantics. I want to do this properly."

He climbed out of the car and walked around to her side. Opening the door, he held his hand out to her. She took it, and no sooner had she gained her feet than she was swept off them. Gallantly, he carried her to the door, and rather than set her down, he tapped the door handle with his foot and nudged the door open with his hip.

"Get a nice breeze up your kilt just now?" she inquired with a wiggle of her brows.

"Yep. And it was worth it." He carried her inside. "I know it's not quite the same as carrying you over the threshold of my cabin because it's not our home, but—"

"It's exactly the same," Celeste interrupted. "Corny

as it might sound, we're home wherever we are as long as we're together."

He kissed her, laughing. "It's corny as hell, but damn, I love you, lass."

"Mmm. Do you, now?"

"I do."

"Prove it."

"Your wish is my command."

He tossed her over his shoulder and headed toward the single bedroom with long strides.

The tiny home above the sea had a timeless, rustic beauty that was both welcomingly similar to the aura of Northstar and enchantingly different. It reminded her of castles and ancient cultures with its native stone walls, rough-hewn timber framing around the doors and windows, the white-washed adornments, and the tiny kitchen, dining room, and living room all squished into one. Antique lamps adorned the walls, but they weren't what provided the soft glow. Dozens of pillar candles—vanilla by the delicious sweetness in the air—had been placed around the space, and flames danced merrily upon their wicks. Even without those and the bouquets of deep red and lavender roses set around the living area and providing the only splashes of rich color, the cottage was wonderfully romantic. She could happily spend weeks sketching in that giant carven armchair beside the window overlooking the undulating sea.

No drawing tonight, she reminded herself as Brodie carried her into the bedroom, cutting off her view of the rest of the cottage. She assuaged the itch with a promise to paint tomorrow afternoon after their reception and outings.

The bedroom was, like the rest of the structure, small and somewhat cramped, but that only made it cozier. Brodie's cousin's had littered the bed with rose petals—both lavender and red—and set out yet more vanilla candles that spiced the air with their fragrance.

"Wow," she said breathlessly.

"You like it?"

"I love it. It's gorgeous."

Brodie settled her on the bed amidst the petals with a gentleness that contrasted the humor still sparkling in his blue eyes. In an unspoken agreement, they began the arduous feat of peeling each other out of their clothing. His kilt, even with all its clasps and buttons required less effort than her dress with its layers of smooth cotton and outer layer of ornate lace. Her fingers trembled in nervousness, and she prayed she didn't rip anything. Finally, she gave up and let Brodie do it. When the dress fell away from her body as if he'd waved a magic wand, she whirled on him and demanded to know how he'd done it.

"Three generations of grooms made sure I knew all its secrets."

The history of the dress and the history of this place enveloped her, and despite her promise not to question or doubt her relationship with Brodie, she couldn't help but hope the dress brought the same strength and longevity to her marriage as it had to the brides who had worn it before her.

At last they stood naked before each other in the writhing light of the candles. Without a breath of hesitation, they embraced, and the touch of skin against skin brought her to the gates of heaven. She exhaled against his shoulder, shivering as he trailed kisses from her jaw to her shoulder. When he scraped his teeth over her skin, tenderness ignited into an inferno of impatient desire. She'd waited over a year for this, and she wasn't going to wait any longer. She latched onto his mouth and kissed him with the intent to devour him.

His throaty chuckle sliced through the haze of desire, and she glared at him.

"It's gone," he croaked.

"What is?"

"That to-hell-with-it recklessness. It's been fading away all year, but now it's completely gone."

"What does that matter?"

"It's the reason I wanted to wait. I wanted us to save this for the moment you wanted it purely for the pleasure of it and not because you were looking for an outlet for your pain and frustration."

Adoration for this man and his amazing, limitless heart swamped her, drowning her irritation at the delay, and her eyes tingled.

"None of that now," he murmured. "I shouldn't have said anything."

"No, I'm glad you did. All this time, I thought you just wanted to save sex for our wedding so it'd be better for the wait, but as it turns out, you were proving once again how incredible you are."

"The light of a spirit like yours makes everything in its beam look beautiful."

"You are definitely that. And stop trying to lift me up, Brodie. I'm already dancing amongst the stars with you."

With Brodie's tender coaxing, that adoration warmed into something much hotter. Seeking caresses turned into fevered strokes as searching fingers explored every inch of skin, memorizing every line and curve. Celeste submitted fully to primal instinct, and sensations flooded her with exquisite intensity. Brodie fumbled with the drawer of the tiny nightstand, and rustling drew Celeste's attention to it.

She burst out laughing. The drawer was brim full of a mind-blowing variety of condoms.

"How many do they think we're going to need?" she asked, still laughing. "Or is that a wedding night joke?"

"Mostly a joke, I expect," Brodie mused. "Inez and our mother might've taught me to see the light in darkness, but I definitely get my sense of humor from my father's side. What's your preference, lass?"

Celeste chewed on her bottom lip. Was she ready to make that decision right now? They'd been together just over a year, and they'd been married less than an hour. Slowly, she replied. "What I want isn't in there."

"Uh, chances are good it is. I don't think I've ever seen this broad a selection outside an adult—"

"I'm certain it isn't in there."

"Take a look if you don't believe me."

She grabbed his hand and yanked him down onto the bed, rolling him onto his back. Confusion hazed his eyes, so she straddled his waist and leaned down to kiss him, sliding her hands up his chest and rocking her hips until he let out a groan. When she pulled away, confusion had given way to understanding and concern.

"Celeste…."

"Shh." She trailed her lips across his chest.

"Don't shush me. I was joking when I told Brendan to let us have tonight if he wanted a sibling."

"I wasn't."

Hope warred with worry in his eyes.

"I know you want a baby, Brodie."

"I do, but I refuse to pressure you into it. That's something that should only happen when *you're* ready."

"I am. That's what I'm trying to tell you. Thanks to you and your patience and love and understanding, I am."

"Tell me why you're so sure."

"You remember what I said to you in your truck the first time I met Steph?"

"I'll never forget it."

"That's how I know. I am safe with you. I have been from the very beginning, and I always will be."

He arched up to kiss her, whispering nonsensically, but she didn't have to comprehend the words to understand their meaning. Love. Gratitude. Hope. Reverence. He stroked and kissed her body until every nerve hummed in anticipation, and then, when she was ready to beg for fulfillment, he pushed into her and the relief of penetration and the promise of release were glorious.

She matched his pace thrust for thrust, angling her hips to take him deeper into her, and let out a cry when he pivoted them and claimed the top. Her body quivered with the passion of their lovemaking, and just before he took her over the edge into sweet oblivion, one final thought splashed across her mind.

This is what it is to be one.

They were united into a single being. One body, one mind, one heart, one soul.

She gasped as the climax peaked and pounded through her. Her body jerked with the force of it, and long after it subsided, the quivers lingered and her breath came and went in pants as her heart thudded against her ribs. Brodie trembled, braced on his forearms above her with his head hanging and a satisfied grin parting his lips. Still joined with him, she pulled his head down to her chest and combed her fingers through his damp auburn hair.

"This," she said breathlessly, "more than any other reason, is why sex should be saved for the wedding night."

"Mmm. Yes. This way truly is consummating our marriage," Brodie murmured. "Sealing it. I obviously didn't believe that before, or I wouldn't have Brendan. But you.… You make me believe a lot of things I never have."

Celeste winced when he pulled away and laid beside her, not ready to break that sense of unity, but minutes passed and the feeling of being one with him remained.

"You weren't the only one running short on hope, lass. I was beginning to believe it was always going to be just Brendan and me. But now we have you." The way he leaned down to press his lips to her belly and then rested his hand there as he settled his head on her shoulder made her heart trip over itself in hope. "And maybe soon we'll have one more to add to our family."

"I hope so." She laughed softly and kissed the top of his head.

Suddenly, he started laughing—a deep, rich belly laugh that seemed to come from the very center of his soul.

"What is so funny?" she asked, smiling helplessly.

"We'd best enjoy this night of being totally alone together, because back home, even when Brendan is at

Steph's, we'll likely have a captive audience."

As the image bounded gleefully into her mind of Bard, Moon, Binx, Jake, and Charlie all gathered around or on the bed while they made love, she joined Brodie in mirth, howling until her sides hurt and her face ached, and it was every bit as marvelous as their joining had been. She didn't expect their life would be roses and candlelight and joy all the time, but she was certain any shadowy moments would be brief and far outnumbered by moments like this.

"Bring it on," she laughed. "All of it."

"All right, you asked for it."

He pounced on her, and she let out of shriek of laughter as he nibbled on her neck.

Still beaming, she sighed, "I guess the stars *do* still have some magic in this world with so little. When I most needed their light, they brought me you."

* * * * *

Don't miss the next book in the *Northstar* **series:**

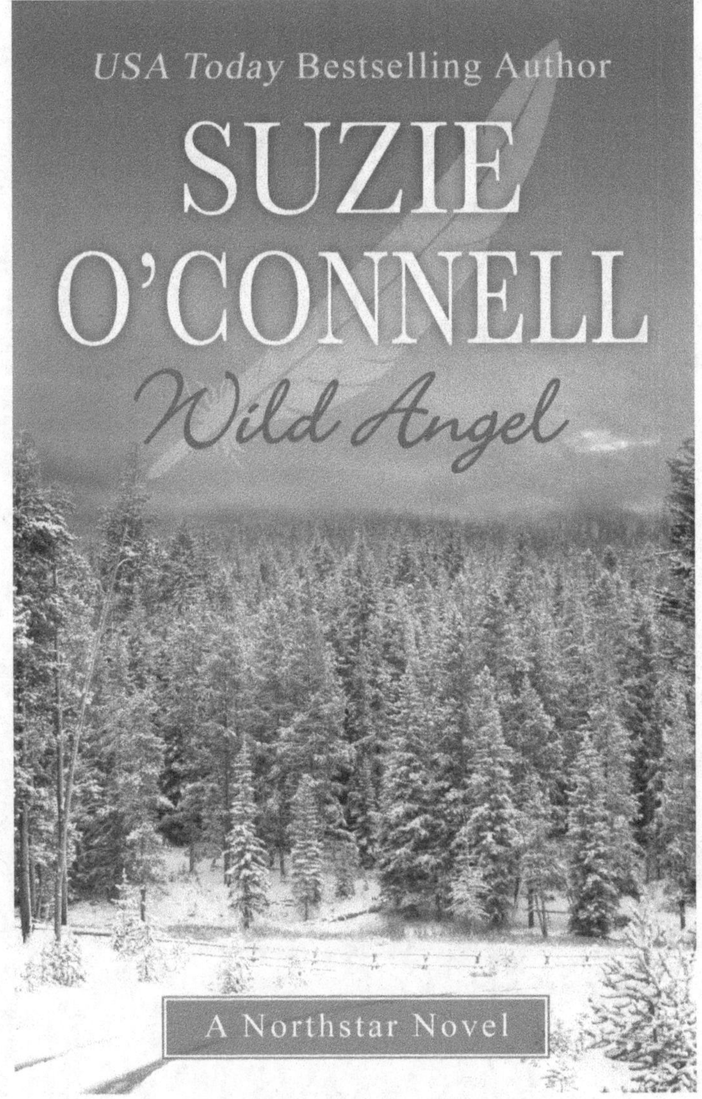

Wild Angel

Everything Luke Conner once wanted from life is slipping away. Ryan Connelly wishes she could be the miracle he needs, but her own heart is still in tatters… and he has ties to the man who broke it.

Ryan and Luke have taught together for four years now, and she's stubbornly ignored the flicker of attraction between them. His friendship—whatever remains of it—with her ex is a complication she doesn't need, but when their colleagues continue to harass him over two murders that happened a decade ago, she can't stay silent anymore.

Ryan's unexpected offer of friendship is a lifeline Luke desperately needs. As he grabs on to it, that spark of attraction flares into something far stronger. Suddenly, Luke finds himself staring at the future he thought was lost to him. But will it last when long-buried secrets are uncovered?

AVAILABLE NOW

Visit www.suzieoconnell.com for more information.

About the Author

Suzie O'Connell is the *USA Today* bestselling author of the Northstar romances. The series is the product of a love affair with Southwestern Montana that began with a two-week adventure at her stepsister's rustic cabin in her teens. That love affair shows no sign of abating.

She has been writing stories for as long as she can remember, and her love of writing and of Montana pushed her to earn a Bachelor of Arts in Literature and Writing from the University of Montana-Western. What else would you expect from a self-professed mountain-loving nerd?

When she isn't writing, you'll probably find Suzie in the mountains with a camera in hand and enjoying the beauty of Montana with her husband Mark, their daughter Maddie, and their golden retrievers Reilly and Angus.

Find Suzie online at www.suzieoconnell.com